Other publications by Alina Loneck

Non-Fiction:

Opals, Rivers of Illusions, Gemcraft publications

ISBN: 978-0-9092232-4-3

Fiction:

Within Sunshine & Shadow, Cilento Publishing

ISBN: 978-0-6450004-4-3

Love is a Many Splendored Thing, Cilento Publishing

ISBN: 978-0-6450004-3-6

Alina's fiction has a rating of 4.7/5 on Amazon Goodreads.

'... compelling reading ... humorous, heart-warming ... challenging and insightful'

'An author who cares about the details'

'Very moving and real. Well-structured and effectively written, revealing feelings, thoughts and reactions that happen to many of us in the world we live in'

I0601117

For the
Love
of *Kieran*
A Novella

Alina Loneck

Alina Loneck asserts the moral right to be identified as the work's author.

This narrative, whilst based upon facts, is a work of fiction. The names of people and places have been changed, fictional characters introduced, and events dramatized.

All rights are reserved.

No part of this publication may be reproduced, stored in a retrieval system or transmitted, in any form or by any means, electronic, mechanical, photocopying, recording, or otherwise, without prior permission from the author.

This book is sold subject to the condition that it shall not, by the way of trade or otherwise, be lent, re-sold, hired out or otherwise circulated without the author's prior consent in any form of binding or cover, other than that, in which it is published and without a similar condition including this condition being imposed on the subsequent purchaser.

Cover and book design Evan Shapiro, Green Avenue Design

ISBN: 978-0-646-85461-8

For the Love of Kieran is dedicated to all those who have loved and lost.
There is not one without the other.

In the end, these things matter most: How well did you love? How fully did you love? How deeply did you learn to let go?

Buddha

Don't give in to your fears.
If you do, you won't be able to talk to your heart.

Paul Coelho, *The Alchemist*

For the Love of Kieran is a work of fiction.
Apart from major cities, all place names are fictional.

Contents

PART ONE
All by Myself   13

PART TWO
The Three of Us   27

Sitting on Top of the World   41

Puppet on a String   51

Around the Bend   61

Baby Come Back   69

Loving Yourself this Christmas   87

Bom Diggy Diggy   95

PART THREE
Stuck in the August Rain   105

Give and Take   127

Time in a Bottle   135

Money, That's What I Want   155

Blacker than Black   161

PART FOUR
With and Without You   173

Ashes   177

ACKNOWLEDGEMENTS   181

PART ONE

All by Myself

Saturday morning breaks clear and crystalline. The space before a February dawn. A space beyond the everyday. He lets go of the breaths he's held all week – one hundred and forty thousand of them – shallow, upper-chest breaths.

He's spent much of his life holding his breath.

As Kieran looks out across Gaagum Creek to the sky beyond, he applies the most accurate weather prediction he knows: watch the ants, and the weather today will be the same as it was the day before. He's right seventy percent of the time.

He's waiting for the rest of the dragon boat crew, a training session at seven. He's got about ten minutes to bring his breathing into the impeccable timing of the row. The astringent tone of the 'What's it to you?' from the night before continues to sting with the bite of a bull ant.

Breathe in for five.

Hold for five.

Out for five

Like a gentle tide rolling to shore, the slow rhythmic flow of the breaths soothes him. Training is one of the few places in his life where he feels calm, has a sense of teamwork and the whispered stirrings of his old strength, courage and belief in himself.

When his breathing settles, he thinks about the legend of the dragon boat and its festival: Qu Yuan, a Chinese hero, and The Warring State Period. After the relatively peaceful Spring and Autumn Period, China's seven leading states battle one another for several hundred years. The Qin State conquers all. Struck by grief at the news, Qu Yuan grabs a large rock and throws himself into the Mi Luo River. Suicide by drowning. Local fishermen launch their boats to recover his body.

Kieran knows what it is to drown. He's spent the last seventeen years disoriented, swallowed whole.

Calmed – adrenals and upper body strength primed – he heads to the designated area. All twenty paddlers are there as well as the drummer. He sees them for the ninety-minute training sessions three times a week: Monday, Wednesday and Saturday. An extended family.

The coach spots Kieran first. "Here he is, lads, Sergeant Sweep."

Kieran is quick to respond. "Good morning, you bunch of latissimi dorsi. I hope you're all carrying your crown jewels dead centre this morning 'cos I don't plan to stand on one leg to hold our course if we're unbalanced."

Jeff is always the first responder with a parry. "Sweep, you should know us all well enough by now to know not only are your crew competitive and focused, but we're all so bloody well-endowed it's not the glide you'll have to worry about; it's a capsize."

"Okay, lads. Let's get this boat in the water. Here's to our blistered and calloused palms."

"Don't forget our arses, too!"

"To *your* bums, *my* bent knees, and *my* vocal cords." His posture from his championship ballroom dancing days is paying dividends now.

They all shout in unison, "To discipline, power and endurance."

When the session finishes, he stays on, as he always does, to train the newbies and the social paddlers. You know the ones. You're in smooth paddling form, and someone loses the sunhat one of their grandkids gave them for their birthday. Sometimes you wonder if you'd be better to throw them overboard with their floatation device, and pick them and their hat up on the return journey. The problem is, he's too much of a gentleman to do that. Then, there's the joker who thinks the commands 'Hold Water' and 'Draw Water' mean rest your paddle on the gunnel, take out your water bottle, and drink.

Sporty since young and obsessed with fitness, Kieran is a natural team player. Since childhood he's been a champion at understanding and applying rules. Rules mean the difference between certainty and fear. They armour him from doing the wrong thing. He knows precisely the commands to prevent a capsize: how to reverse or turn a boat around, stop the paddlers and float gently to a destination. How, in a competition, to readjust a boat's course when another boat underestimates the designated thirty metres of separation and veers towards them.

So, *why the hell* is it like herding wild cats to stop or slow what's happening at home? It's impossible to navigate around the obstacle that is his wife. If there are rules, they are incomprehensible because they always seem to be changing. No matter how he readjusts his course, he can never seem to please Renata. She's either unmoved or moved to rage. But he'll never say a bad word against her. One of his rules is that a gentleman never speaks ill of anyone. At home, he feels powerless, weak, faint-hearted, sluggish. At the moment, his only two proven floatation devices to keep his body and mind above water are his sports (boating and soccer) and his weekly appointment with a psychologist.

It's ten a.m. by the time Kieran heads back to the house. Renata will be shopping and having a coffee catch-up with friends that often extends into lunch.

At home the only note his wife has left, magnetized to the fridge, is a computer-generated to-do list for their investment unit at Bellows Beach, twenty minutes south, that they run as a B&B. It was easier when their only child, Max, lived in the apartment before moving to Melbourne. Hard to believe he's almost thirty.

Kieran opens the fridge door. Power smoothie time: kale, sugar banana, fresh raspberries, raw egg, ginger, a tablespoon of coconut oil and two tablespoons of protein powder, one Nutribullet. He downs it, cleans up after himself, grabs the note, loads up his Subaru Forester and heads out.

Oh, yes. He has two other strategies to avoid discomfort and pain in life. The ones he's always had – keep busy, keep fit. Both act as a panacea for stress and tension. The combo worked perfectly in his thirties, but at sixty-four it's not succeeding. It's far easier to command acquaintances on the water than it is to deal with personal confrontation in the kitchen. Conflict is all there is now since he and his wife live in their own permanent 'stay-in-your-own-section' lockdown. The rare nights of making love to a log and post-coital turned backs are long gone. Thoughts and feelings are masked – his, not hers. An arm's length distance applies at all times. Heartbreakingly easy to do in a large split-level waterfront home.

When he returns home, he's exhausted. He grabs a snack from the fridge and heads to his quarters. His television has become a Time Vaporizer he switches on as soon as he gets in, and before he knows it, it's bedtime. Tonight, his eyelids droop. He drifts. Plummets. His limbs twitch as he drops off to sleep on the recliner. On a good night, the anaesthesia of sleep blots out everything.

Kieran has long given up the Rubik's Cube that Renata's become. No matter which way he twists and turns to please and appease her, he can never get it right. To be in his wife's presence is to commit an invisible crime. They haven't made love for two years. He can only fix what he can – Tuesdays – the only blank space in his weeknights. A night with four walls, takeaway pizza, beer and Spotify. Thursdays, Renata's out at salsa. Kieran discovers a Tuesday rock 'n' roll class at the local RSL. Perfect – rules, action. Also, the chance to hold a woman's hand and to firmly, but gently, lead her and have her follow.

The first thing Marianne notices when she turns up for Tuesday's rock 'n' roll lesson is a man sitting on the far fringes of the line of chairs that flank the tables with seats that hug the edges of the parquet dance floor. The man sits with a schooner of beer for company. He's slim and good-looking in a rugged way, but she's too far away to say hello. She makes her way to her circle of dance friends who always seat themselves alongside the dance floor. There's her closest friend, Ana, a widow for ten years. Ana and her husband, Steve, were so in tune that she still feels him around her. She's very open about having an occasional chat with him. She's known as the 'Duracell Bunny', not only because she's a coppertop – a redhead – but also because she has six times the energy of any other woman on the dance floor. At the socials, Ana outlasts even the most robust of partners to the point where they disappear to the bar or the loo. Some pray that their mates will rescue them by asking her to dance. Ana, she'll make it well into her hundreds *still* doing the shake, rattle and roll with someone half her age. Ana is keen on Dan; he reminds her of Steve. He's tall, lean, dark-haired, good-looking and always polite and pleasant. Unfortunately, in his mid-fifties, Dan is only attracted to women three decades younger. How's that working out for him? Not okay. 'Another one bites the dust' and 'lonely days'. Some people never learn.

There's Meg and Chris who have only just begun dating. She's a single mum and works in aged care, and Chris works as a courier. Chris doesn't say a lot, but Meg accepts that about him because he's steady, a fabulous dancer and great with her two young kids. Meg doesn't mind at the socials if Chris dances with other women. He's not a flirt, far from it, but he has an intense quiet kindness that notices the unpartnered women and fixes it. There are two or three guys from the Tuesday group like that.

Then, there's Corrine, a sports physio, who lives to dance, married to a great guy who won't. Maybe it's a two left feet thing.

Finally, Rachel, Joanne, Alice, Caroline, Lydia, Rod, Jeff and Aaron. All single and looking for love on the dance floor or, at the very least, companionship, touch, and a workout twisting and smiling a few hours away.

The only one with an absent smile is the newcomer – the man with the beer.

The format of the lesson is a relay: a couple of practises of a new move and then a rotation clockwise to the next partner.

When the newcomer rotates to Marianne, she's struck by how much he resembles her dad: grey hair, kind eyes, similar height and build. As they practise 'The Promenade', the *leave me in my shell* is physically palpable; although, his posture does not betray it. When he thanks her for the dance and briefly makes eye contact, she notices that his blue eyes are full of sadness. From nowhere, a single word pops into her head. Broken. He is a broken man – the walking wounded. Privately, she nicknames him Mister Summertime Blues.

At the end of the class, he leaves straightaway. The entire night he's only said a thank you to one woman – Marianne.

On the third Tuesday, Marianne finishes work early on reception at All Connected, a private ENT practice. There's been a last-minute end of day cancellation. Her boss, Scott, is good like that; he does his best to make up for the days when he has to slip in an urgent last-minute patient. His mother the practice manager is an entirely different cup of tea. She's the sort of woman who uses the same teabag three times, and the staffroom biscuits are always from out-of-date packets tipped into a metal-clipped glass jar that keeps the hand, forearm and thumb in top muscular condition. The label on the jar says, 'One cup of tea, one biscuit.' Every time Marianne sees the six words, her mind replaces them with five: 'Reach out, I'll be there.' Thereupon, she takes an extra biscuit ... or two. Marianne wonders why Scott allows his mother to behave this way towards staff. Either his focus is on higher matters, or he's in cahoots with his mum to keep the budget on track and his frontline workers looking trim and terrific. Marianne would bet her second biscuit that it's the first reason.

Marianne heads straight from work to the club. She tells herself there's no point driving the fifteen minutes home and fifteen minutes back. As the monumental glass doors of the club open for her, she heads straight to the female toilets on the right. They are oh-so chic. A glass-framed void behind the continuous sink houses luscious green ferns of different sizes. The sink is a clinical-white ceramic slab that slopes backwards to the stainless-steel architectural drain at the rear. Motion sensors activate the taps. She hasn't come in to use the loo. She's come to put on lip gloss and fluff her hair. After leaving the toilets, she heads to the main desk to sign in, then past the restaurant and pokies to the dance area.

There he is.

A still life shot as every other week, even down to the level of creamy froth on his beer.

No one else is there apart from the bartender. Marianne heads towards Mister Summertime Blues.

"Hi, I'm Marianne. I could do with some company. May I sit with you till the others arrive?"

He nods.

"So, what's your name and what's your story? Are you married or what?"

It's so direct, he flinches. A breath halts mid-way. It never occurs to him not to answer, to deflect by asking a question.

Marianne manages to get away with her directness because there's an innocent, childlike air and soft gentility about her – no hint of the huntress. She's five feet to his five foot ten, petite yet curvaceous, wears little make-up, flat pumps, and her hair is shoulder length and curly. It's the warmth and twinkle in her eyes, the smile and slight laugh in her voice that make him relax. He's not under threat.

"I'm Kieran. Kieran Campbell. And yes, I'm married."

"How come your wife's not here?"

"My wife doesn't enjoy rock 'n' roll. She does salsa instead. And you?"

"I'm married too, but my husband won't dance. He's a bit of a stay-at-home, and– Oh, the others are here. You're quite welcome to join us."

"I'm fine, thank you."

They part with an identical feeling, private secrets floating below the surface of what each has said. He's suffering, and she's suffocating.

As the weeks pass, they develop an intimate knowledge of each other. Marianne can see in his eyes that his Tuesday blues have become the beginnings of a friendship. Both discover their situations are similar. Two couples. Two homes. Separate lives. The only difference is that her in-house withdrawal has only been six months, with no animosity (like brother and sister), a breakdown with a fizzle rather than an explosion.

Something is happening between Marianne and Kieran, something delightful. Kieran can't remember when he'd last felt *seen* by a woman. "I don't know how you do it, but I'm always amazed how I am able to open up to you, Marianne. I feel completely safe around you. I don't think you're the sort of woman to play games."

"I'm not. If we spend more time together, I hope you'll discover that. I think I probably push you to the point where you have no choice but to open up. I'll warn you, I have a mild exterior and am shy, believe it or not, but at the same time, I am very sociable and, at times, pushy. I'm still working on the balance. My boss calls me Little Miss Meticulous 'cos I'm so organised and efficient at work. Do you have a nickname?"

"I have a few. It depends on who you talk to."

"That sounds intriguing. Tell me more."

"My close friends call me The Great Procrastinator because I can find it hard to make decisions. As an architect, I always finish projects ahead of time, so the guys at the office call me The Terminator. The dragon boaters call me sarge because as sweep, I'm in charge of the boat and their safety."

"That leaves me a bit short. I'll have to work on a few more pet names."

"I can add one, but I don't really know you well enough – Baby. You're very similar in looks to Frances from *Dirty Dancing*, twenty-five years on."

"That's a great movie. Yes, I remember that's what Johnny called her ... I know, I've got a nickname for us both – Swayze and Grey. You do have a bit of the Patrick Swayze look about you. How old are you anyway?"

This time he deflects. "That's for me to know and–"

"I know, I know. For me to find out. Don't worry. I will."

He's worried that she won't be interested in him when she finds out how old he is.

She persuades him to come to the dance socials on the occasional Friday after soccer practice or if it's cancelled. They become dance partners. He is happy to go with the flow, but she has decided to pursue him with gentle tenacity.

As their conversations deepen over the month, Marianne starts to dream at night, not about Kieran but about her dad. Her adored dad died of prostate cancer at sixty-seven. Marianne's daughter, Molly, was only five and her son, Liam, a month premature.

In one dream, Marianne is asking Liam, "What have you been doing, mate?"

"Playing with Grandpa."

"Playing what?"

"Paper. Scissors. Rock."

It's one-thirty in the morning, and Marianne wakes heavy-headed and laden with guilt from the dream. Her dad had played the game with her as a child, but she'd never shared it with Liam. It's a dream of a memory. The memory of Liam as a young child playing and chattering to his grandpa in his bedroom, a photo of Pops in an army uniform by his bedside. How that boy loved action figures. At the time, Marianne thought maybe she talked too much about her dad. He had been sick for some time when cancer was discovered. After the diagnosis, he had eight months of living left. She couldn't care for him, as she had demanding work and family committments. Regret stabs deep. Sometimes timing is shit.

Marianne falls back to sleep. This time it's Liam, aged two. Marianne's dad is bouncing him up and down on his leg to a daft ditty from his 1950s childhood:

"I tiddley-i-tie eat, brown bread!

I saw a sausage fall down dead.

Up came a butcher with a great big knife.

Up jumped the sausage and ran for his life.

Hi-tiddley-i-tie, brown bread."

It didn't happen to Liam.

It happened to Marianne.

'Ghost Riders in the Sky'.

Her dad's favourite Marty Robbins's song.

PART TWO

The Three of Us

By early March, Kieran and Marianne have swapped addresses. One Friday night after dancing, he offers to drive her home. On the way, he parks at the headland overlooking the bay, and there they cuddle and kiss like teenagers at a drive-in.

"I can see us being perfect for one another as well as being good to each other. I promise I will never mistreat you, be mean to you, deceive you or intentionally make you mad, sad or alone."

Mistreated, sad, alone. Kieran is all of these. The hurt from Renata's morning eye roll, her favourite gesture, lodges in his chest as if it were a clenched fist.

To Marianne, these are the sun streaming times. She wants him to be happy, to jump off the cliff and find his wings on the way down. She has no idea how terrifying that thought is for him because not to do so is incomprehensible to her – life is too short not to be happy.

"You've got no idea how it is at home. It's not that easy."

She embraces him, holds him and says, "No, hun, I don't. So, how about you tell me."

"The first ten years or so were fine. Renata was doting and loving. I don't know why it changed, and I didn't know how to put it right. I've been going to a psychiatrist on and off for years. He tells me I need to do something about it, as it's destroying me."

"What's making it difficult for you to walk away?"

"It just feels too hard – overwhelming. How do I do it in a way that doesn't alienate my son and minimises the fallout from Renata? She'll fight tooth and nail to ensure she has the lion's share of what we own. I've worked too hard to build what I have now. I can't do it."

Marianne backs off, as she can feel the anxiety rise in him like hot water poured into a cold teapot. She gets him. He has his own timing. Be patient, Marianne. Good things come to those who wait.

She focuses on the upcoming weekend away, dancing to the music of 'Rock-a-Hula' at Langaratta RSL. There's a group going from the dance class. She's booked a room with Ana. Kieran has booked a single room, as the only other uncoupled male going is Dave and he snores. Dave also knows Renata.

Marianne texts Kieran on the prior Wednesday. *Busy day today – hairdresser, facial and pedicure. I am looking forward to the weekend. Pack your swimmers. They have a pool and spa. I'll bring wine.*

There's an immediate response; he must have been sitting on his phone. *That sounds dangerous: people in swimmers, a pool, a spa, a bottle of wine. I think I may need to book in for a bikini wax.*

You're a funny man! We're going to have lots of fun.

Fun? He's unsure what she means by that. *Should I be worried about all this fun we are going to have?*

A message swoops back. *Don't let your mind get too carried away.*

She's taken his text the wrong way. He'd better make himself clear. *The mind doesn't get too carried away, as I just go with the flow.*

'Go with the flow?' She doesn't know what to make of him sometimes. Is he interested or not? She's getting mixed messages. In one text, he mentions her beautiful eyes, that he wants to hold her close and dance his heart out. Two kisses. Sometimes, it's just a kiss and a hug. He texts he's interested, but sometimes his actions don't match his words.

At the end of the first night away, Marianne and Kieran talk and cuddle in his room into the early hours of Saturday morning. His kisses find their way to the soles of her feet, curl her toes and melt her heart. When she sneaks back to her room, Ana is fast asleep, snoring.

Ana is still comatose when Marianne goes down for the buffet breakfast.

Marianne spots Kieran eating alone and sits next to him. She apologises for the passionate kiss she gave him when they left the club at the end of the previous night's dancing.

"I came on too strong. It was impulsive of me. I'm sorry."

"Hey, you don't need to apologise, except perhaps to Ana. She looked appalled. I encouraged you, and I enjoyed it. It did catch me off-guard though, as I didn't expect a passionate kiss in Ana's presence. If Renate hears that we're more than dance partners, it will be a war zone at home when I get back."

"Are you worried Dave will say something?"

"He wasn't there when you kissed me, so there's nothing to tell; just a group having a good time dancing. What he does say should support my version of the night. Renata's no fool; she'll piece things together. Even Pete, my neighbour at home, is starting to think 'dance partner' is a euphemism for something else.

Ana is awake and furious when Marianne returns to their room.

"Dance partners, my arse! Kieran's still married and so are you. *You are dating a married man.* And don't give me the spiel about how your marriages are over so it doesn't matter. *It does.* Renata is still his wife, and Adam is still your husband. You can't be in a romantic relationship. Separate bedrooms *do not* mean separated. Show some respect. Do it when you've both made a clean break. You've no idea about Kieran's past. How do you know he's not just stringing you along? Even supposedly lovely guys want to have their cake and eat it."

"That's *so* inappropriate of you to say that."

"Really! Do you know what *is* appropriate? To remind you, under ten percent of affairs lead to men leaving their wives. Most affairs never last past the excitement and adoration stage of falling in love. He's got unfinished business, or he'd have arranged a divorce years ago. Either way, you've got a hard road ahead of you."

Marianne looks sobered but defiant. She knows that if Kieran has the courage to leave, there will be a bitter road to divorce, and, one way or another, it will entangle her.

"You're jealous I'm with Kieran, as you'd like to have that with Dan. You can't bear seeing someone else in a romantic relationship when you don't have one yourself."

Ana is stunned and wounded. "How could you think that! I'm the first to be overjoyed if any of my friends meet someone. You've chosen to interpret love and concern from a friend as envy."

"Anyway, it's none of your business!"

"Look here, Marianne. It became my business when you slobbered all over him in front of me. He's not single. He's not available. You need to run."

It's seven o'clock on the Saturday night, and it's rocking at Langaratta RSL. The group, minus Ana, are sitting at one long table. The awkward impasse between Ana and Marianne is solved: Ana has found a dance partner who's a local. He invites her to sit at the table with his group of friends. Both Ana and Marianne are relieved they don't have to sit in close proximity, each with their cold fury.

Kieran is spreading himself around as there are, as always, too many women. He asks Lydia for a dance. She was his dance partner for ballroom before he took up rock 'n' roll. She's Greek-Dutch heritage and sexy: slim, attractive, dark wavy hair, delicate features and great poise on the dance floor. She seems to have it all in the attraction stakes till she opens her mouth. She'd never make a living as a phone sex operator. Her voice has a pingy quality, high tones mixed with low tones and harsh spat-out consonants. Kieran and Lydia are all eye contact and smiles; he continues to hold onto her hand when the song finishes, touching her arm as he speaks to her at the edge of the dance floor before they return to their separate seats. Marianne's 'incoming female' antennae are up.

Marianne fishes. "He's a great dancer, isn't he? You two dance so well together. You can always tell the couples on the floor who have been long-term dance partners."

"I was the love of his life – a soulmate."

Marianne's paralysed. Oh, my god. He'd never make the first move, but …

As the group dawdles back to the hotel at the night's end, she lags behind next to Kieran.

"Kieran, you're such a lovely guy, and I'm attracted to you in a big way, but after chatting briefly with Lydia and seeing the connection between you two tonight, I'm beginning to think I'm a third wheel. I'm feeling cautious about opening my heart to you." She tells him what she saw, what Lydia said.

There's a micro-tilt of Kieran's head, an arched eyebrow and widening eyes indicating, *'Surely,* you don't believe that!' "*She* said that. *Not me.* Look, It's my wife that's the issue. Lydia is not. There's no way I'd have a relationship with Lydia – emotional dynamite. I have plenty of problems without another volatile woman in my life. Three women would be impossible." Then he gently, and without emotion, adds, "If cautious is where you're at, that's perfectly fine by me."

Langaratta is turning into the weekend from hell.

Marianne's glad when Sunday morning arrives, and she and the others head home. Marianne needs to work out if Kieran's a gentleman or a player. Is there such a thing as a gentleman player? She stops and thinks … sure there is. You know the ones, gentlemen on the surface but man-sluts below the belt. Is Kieran terrified to draw close emotionally because he's learnt it brings confusion and pain? She stops answering his texts.

There's no room in anyone's car for Marianne to go back home in other than Ana's. The two of them spend the four-hour trip in silence, apart from curt replies for the necessities.

When Ana drops Marianne home, she says, "Please, Marianne, think about what I said. I don't want you caught in the middle of someone's *War of the Roses* movie-style divorce. It'll be all dark, no comedy."

"I agree. The kiss wasn't appropriate. I apologise. I just got carried away in the moment – one drink too many. And yes, I was unfair to you, but I know Kieran. He may be a procrastinator when it comes to leaving his wife, but he *is* a gentleman."

Ana wants to say, "Are you sure of that?" However, she knows, if she doesn't want to lose the friendship, she needs to keep her mouth shut and her door open. "Okay, friend. Let's leave it there. We've both said our piece. I won't bring it up again. Just don't ever involve me again as a bystander."

On Monday morning at five-thirty, there's a message alert on Marianne's phone. Her heart misses a beat. It's Kieran.

Sorry about Saturday. I really think I've blown this. I have had no romantic relationship while I have been in my marriage. Goodnight. Late. 🩶 *xo xo xo*

Wow, doesn't he know he's digging himself a deeper hole? Romantic? Is it a Clinton and Monica Lewinsky moment? 'I did not have sexual relations with that woman.'

When Marianne fails to respond to Kieran's message, he texts her. *Look, if you need to walk away, I will respect your decision. But please, stay friends.*

No response.

He takes a deep breath and types. *Aren't you talking to me? Please text. I am trying hard.*

Still no response.

He's now in pleading mode. *What do I need to do for you to talk? Talk to me. Please. It's never been about wanting sex with you. It's been about the relationship.*

As dusk begins to drop and shadow, Marianne re-evaluates her position. Poor man. She knows he must be feeling sick to the pit of his stomach. He desperately needs the joy her friendship brings. She's a safe haven, a refuge for a miserable man. He *really is* trying hard. She just ... just wishes Kieran would focus on where he wants to go, instead of where he is now and where he has been. She can't understand why he is so invested in a failed enterprise.

Marianne decides to own her power but remember her heart. At two in the morning, she texts him. *I needed time to think. Let's put the break on until we are both clear on where this is heading. But believe me, I can see us making very passionate love in the future.*

A few seconds later her phone pings.

When the time comes, I will not be able to resist. I dream of it. Did anyone tell you that you looked gorgeous last night?

Hi, handsome. No, nobody did.

Well, I should have. You looked great, but my dancing was terrible because I was too busy looking into your eyes. A guy on

the news the other day. A hundred and three and still dancing.
Pencil me in on your dance card for the year 2056!

He is the sweetest and most transparent of men; he hasn't realised he's inadvertently told her how old he is. Sixty-five to her fifty-six. Truth be told, she's more interested. Age is just a number. He reminds her so much of her dad, who's worked his celestial magic to bring Kieran to her. Love you, Dad.

Marianne doesn't play games, but she is a strategist. Her advice to herself is to back off a little and put herself back in charge; a woman can get what she wants without always stating desires directly. She's not going to wait around while Kieran decides if he wants to be with her or not. She books a cruise for mid-June; the date his wife will be away for a few weeks in The Maldives with girlfriends. Marianne gathers Renata is more a cocktail and cruise person than climbing and canoeing, team talks rather than team sports.

Kieran's response? "You're certainly a go-getter. No moss on the soles of your shoes."

"I believe we all have a choice, and we are the only ones to control that. We only have ourselves to blame if we don't make the right choices to care for our happiness. You only get one chance at life. You don't drown by falling into the water unless you stay there."

"Look, Mara Mia, I'm trying to clear the air with Renata and sort things out around moving out and splitting our assets. The debates are lengthy and heated. Any argument I put forward is quickly rebuffed with, 'You're missing the point, *as usual.*' She always goes back to when we first got together – the no-frills registry marriage. We'd both agreed it was better to use our money to secure a home. She is also a master at twisting any points I put forward that highlight she's possibly wrong; she resets them to further confirm her point of view. It's like arguing with a steel door. My brain is mush because she confuses me with half-truths and processes emotions fast. I feel pushed into a corner with no say in the outcome. I try to de-escalate the conflict by walking away when I feel my blood pressure and pulse rise and the tremor in my hands. There's no safe place to speak up and say my piece. I listen. I say nothing. Please, Marianne, be patient with me. I *will* be heard."

"Remember, my sweet man, you have a voice and a choice. I will have to teach you to be more assertive. Looking forward to tender passion when the timing is right."

"Sorry, I'm downloading on you. It's been a downer of a day. I deal with constant criticism, but it's only on some occasions that it gets to me. Glad I've got the training for the upcoming Dragon Boat Nationals. Smashed shoulders will take my mind off things."

Kieran's life at home is a storm. He wakes to flawless blue skies that, within seconds, cloud over to bruise the day. Renata's thunder and pelting, pummelling words flay like piercing shards of glass. However, unlike a passing storm, the sun doesn't come back above 4, Maralinga Close.

After the phone call, Marianne sends him a text – an affirmation. *Happy Tuesday. Remember to say, I am loveable, I am loving, I am loved.*

Kieran smiles when he reads it. *You are so supportive. Thanks for being a friend and, most of all, for being you.*

What's it with 'friend' again?

Vulnerable, she texts back. *Do you miss me?*

I certainly do! My day's brighter when I read your texts. I just want to be with you. Goodnight, beautiful. xxxooo

Warmed and reassured that he misses her and wants to be with her, she responds with, *Maybe we have been brought together so I can help you through this. I believe some people come into our lives when we need them most. It might only be for a short time. Whatever I can do to help, I am here.*

However, his moving on and off the fence is a constant challenge for her. It's certainly not the time to tell him she tingles at his touch. He's scared. It was always just comfortable with Adam, even from the start. They'd been childhood friends, and the timing had been right. She'd had enough of the single life; marriage and kids seemed appealing. She loved mothering but not the monotony of same old, same old.

Mid-autumn and Ana's shedding what no longer serves her – lost boys. She gives up on Peter Pan Dan and his girls. She's ready to explore a relationship with Grant, who she met at Langaratta. It's the only positive thing that came out of that feuding friend's weekend. With Grant there's an easy connection on and off the dance floor. Her friends think he's fabulous. He lives four hours away. Ana's more his way than hers because the dancing and bands are better where he lives.

Ana plans to visit Grant the first weekend in April. She asks Marianne to look after the house and her little boxer, Houdini.

You don't need a house number to know where Ana lives. It's the only fence on the street that required planning permission. The entire street, and the postman, believe Houdini is a cross between an undomesticated dog and an octopus – wild, intelligent and boneless. He's an insistent and creative escapee from the backyard.

Kieran stays over on the Friday night of the house-sit. It's two months since he and Marianne met, but he still hasn't told his wife about their relationship. Marianne has already let her husband know that she's seeing a male friend. Rather he hears it from her than from someone else. She wishes Kieran would do the same.

Marianne tries a new tack. "Why doesn't Renata leave?"

"Not sure. Possibly finances. Renata says she has no feelings for me anymore. She is talking about separation. She's gone back to using her maiden name and has opened a separate account."

"Look, babe, why waste your life being unhappy. It sounds as if you are both driven by finances and the fear of not having enough or losing it all, but material things don't make for happiness."

Kieran rubs the space between his eyebrows. He can feel the painful pulse of a headache building. "Look, Marianne, I'm not doing this today. Just leave it. I'm barely coping with one woman on my case, never mind two. I'm off to buy beer."

Ironically, his favourite beer is 'One Fifty Lashes'.

Pete is picking up his weekly supply of Toohey's Dry when Kieran arrives at the bottle-o. Pete and Kieran have been neighbours and close friends for twenty-five years.

"Hi, mate. Not one of your blue suede shoe nights?"

"No, Pete, not till tomorrow night. Music from the fifties to seventies with the band, 'The Cadillacs'. Always a great night."

"I bet. At our age, us men outnumber women about twenty to one on the dance floor. Shame I've got two left feet."

Pete suspects Kieran is seeing someone, but he's not one to pry. If you ask Pete about Renata, he says only good things: what a kind neighbour she is; how she's always the first with a lift or a meal when you're unwell. But Pete *knows* the situation at home. He'll never forget when Renata humiliated Kieran at the soccer Christmas party by dancing with everyone else but her husband. The time she emptied a bucket of ice in Kieran's lap at an Italian restaurant. Pete never did find out what that was all about. He and Kieran would have a chuckle over it without malice because, ironically, the restaurant's name was *La Cozca Infuriata* – The Angry Mussel. Renata certainly carries a lot of muscle when she's mad. Her anger is never *al dente*. When it comes to Kieran and her sharing a meal, Kieran is best advised to *mangia e zitto* – eat and keep silent! Reckon though, you never know with Renata when it comes to Kieran, the outcome could prove as dangerous as a lit match near a petrol spill – corrosive, flammable and toxic. Conflicts between nations, never mind people, can start for the most preposterous reasons – pigs, a stray dog, a severed ear, pastry. Battles not taught about at school.

Pete has tried to have a word with Kieran about Renata, but his, 'Mate, you *really* need to leave her.' was met with an, 'It's not so easy.' and a change of topic. Pete wonders if he should have a word with Kieran about flypaper. Pete's a confirmed bachelor. He knows all about flypaper.

Flypaper. The old-fashioned way of catching flies. You'd buy it in a box with the ribbons coiled inside. You'd unwind the sweet, sticky film and dangle it to attract those buzzing bastards that regurgitate wherever they land. It's like nectar to a bee. The fly lands for a taste. Happy, it settles on the honeyed trap and laps up all that's on offer. O*ooh, so nice.* Without lifting a wing, it's found a soft warm home and convenient snacks. However, when it tries to fly free, there's no going anywhere. Days of exploring other à la carte ribbon adventures are over. He pines for those days when his wings trembled, his soul soared. The hairs on the fly's back prickle with restlessness and fear. He has to risk everything – his energy, his life – if he wants to free himself from the film that binds. That flypaper wants *all* of the fly to itself – *forever*. But all that fly desires is to explore all those irresistible sweet ribbons. No ribbon is a fly-by-night rendezvous. Dance partners? Fair dinkum!

There's no more talk about Renata when Kieran returns with the beer. Just mentioning her name brings up a video in his mind of the morning two years ago, the day of their wedding anniversary, when he noticed her naked finger. Rings on the tree of marriage gone – engagement, wedding, eternity. Hope and possibility – gone. Connection to heart – gone. Barely able to breathe because the absence was there for all to see, the piercing bareness and shame of it caught on his heart like thorns against bare flesh. He was now an outcast from a club, the rules of which most of his mates had mastered.

"What will I say if anyone asks?"

A victorious smile had played on the edge of Renata's lips and a stare that could cut concrete. "You can tell them what you want. It's of no interest to me."

The cool toxicity of her remark reduced him to silence.

Sitting on Top of the World

Kieran is grateful that he and Marianne are watching the movie *Tinker Tailor Soldier Spy*. Gary Oldman is one of his favourite actors. It's a terrific spy thriller, and he hasn't watched it since it came out in 2011. She's paired the DVD with two of his other favourites: Lindt dark chocolate with hazelnuts and a bottle of Chivas Regal. She's such a sweetie. He doesn't have to think or talk. They lean into one another on the sofa chaise, their feet touching. The cuddles and closeness soothe and settle Kieran. For Marianne, they make her feel loved.

Within a couple of weeks, Ana's away again for the weekend. Marianne is to look after home and Houdini. As she and Kieran prepare Friday night's dinner, they are as close as two people can be. It's a tiny kitchen.

He asks her, "Can you cook and kiss at the same time?"

"I am more into constant kissing than I am cooking. Have I lost your heart already?"

"No, but I have just the strategy to add some spice to the cookpot that doesn't involve chilli or paprika."

In the golden glow of the candle light, Kieran watches mesmerised as Marianne stirs the pot on the stove with careful circular strokes. So smooth. So slow. So calm. He comes up behind her – no degree of separation. She feels his hands gently stroke her bare shoulders. She can smell the aromatic virile notes of his, 'black is mysteriously masculine', Trussardi Uomo cologne – basil, cinnamon, patchouli. She smiles, closes her eyes, takes a deep breath and slightly tilts her head to the left. Gently, he brushes her fragrant curls to one side to reveal her bare neck. She exhales, slow and deep. His hands back on her shoulders, she feels the warmth of his breath over the nape of her neck. He leans his lips next to her ear and whispers, "*I've missed you.*" His lips hover over the silky surface of her neck, sending sweet spasms through her body – eroticism, vulnerability and surrender. As he kisses her neck, indescribable tingles shiver through her body. Her breath quickens as Kieran slides his hands to the place where her ribcage softens into her breasts. All Marianne wants is for this moment to last forever.

After finishing a candlelit dinner, both feel nervous – willing, curious, uncertain. Bare, naked, unshielded desire for the unexplored always involves risk. Marianne hasn't made love to Adam for a year and Kieran to Renata, two.

"I know it's not the ideal place, but by late May, early June, I should finalise things between Adam and me, and I can look for a villa. A love nest for two."

"Building a relationship with you is what matters most to me, knowing that you are your own person, and I can trust you implicitly. I've shared things with you I've never shared with anyone before."

"You're just the sweetest man. It's hard not to love you."

He says, "You're a fantastic woman I like and admire." He thinks, *one step at a time ... let the pace set itself.*

Marianne wishes the last word was desire. It's obvious the chemistry is there on both sides. Is it just he is not the best at expressing his emotions in words? She's sure that's it. Marianne hopes her settlement with Adam will prompt Kieran to do the same. Mind you, Adam is a different kettle of fish. When it's raining, he rehouses stray huntsmen spiders to more suitable indoor accommodation (the garage) using the base of a takeaway container and a sheet of A4 cardboard – that's *like* and *admire.*

In the candlelit bedroom, she and Kieran undress each other slowly. Marianne delights in the places where her smoothness meets the hairs on his chest and arms. They fall together, his chest solid against the softness of her breasts. She yields to the union of the weight of his body upon hers.

He's aroused, but she's aware as he lies on top of her that his penis is like uncooked dough. There is no seize and thrust. She opens her eyes. He is watching her – isolated, anxious. She smiles, draws his head close to hers, and looking into his eyes, she glides his two victory fingers along the slip and suck of her tongue and dewy lips. Then, she guides his right hand to the moist warmth of her vagina. On her back, her body arches and she strangles his wrist to a stop with both her hands. "Stop. Stop. I am *so* close." Within minutes – her feet ballerina-pointed and every muscle in her legs taut – she bursts wide open with primal, guttural rising vowels. His penis tingles, and a drop of fluid hangs at the semi turgid tip.

Her torso flushes with a warm surge of contentment as she coos lazily, "That was so delicious. Thank you. Your timing and rhythm were spot on. I am one satisfied woman."

"I'm sorry about my penis not rising to the occasion. I think it's normal in men my age. A case of not too fast, not too slow. Just not at all."

"Not necessarily; besides, you're so fit."

"I may need to get Viagra?"

She laughs that beautiful warm tinkling laugh of hers. "Don't you dare. For a start, I don't think I am up for four hours of non-stop sex, and I won't know when you blush, whether you're embarrassed or horny."

"Assume the latter."

"Noted! We do need to check it out, though. Possibly a blockage."

"Are you talking doctors here, or plumbers?"

She hits him with the feather pillow.

He disarms her, pulls her to him and whispers, "I'm a lover, not a fighter."

"*Boy*, do I know *that*. You just have to look at me, touch me, whisper in my ear, and I'm all electrical surges."

As they fall asleep, a warm contented lubricious tenderness enfolds them. Marianne knows what he has a fondness for, so she strokes the soft skin of his inner arm, and when she turns, he caresses her back as she falls asleep. She spoons him when they turn again, and her hand cups his penis. Her breasts press against the warmth of his back and her belly against the curve of his bottom. So divine to stir in the early hours and find his lips instead of a text, to feel the rhythm of her breath in unison with his.

In the morning, Kieran's up early for dragon boat training. A six forty-five start. On the water at seven. Marianne is still dozing in bed when she hears Kieran's smooth baritone voice in the shower singing a Beach Boys' version of 'Do You Want to Dance?'.

'Do you, do you, do you ...' Yes, she does. She wants to dance and hold Kieran's hand under the moonlight. She wants to hold and kiss her lover man all through the night. She drifts back to sleep, and on waking she rolls over, forgetting the bed will be empty of him. Well almost. There's a note and his shirt from the night before.

Sorry about the empty space beside you. Here's a little bit of me till I see you on Sunday, my beautiful lady. Good luck with your villa hunting at the open for inspections today. Don't overdo it at the gym. xoxoxo

At seven o'clock in the evening, Marianne texts Kieran. There's no response. Is he ghosting her? Is he embarrassed and ashamed because he couldn't sustain an erection the night before? She didn't make a big deal of it. Their lovemaking had been so satisfying and sensual: the union of their bare flesh and the intoxicating spicy woodiness of his armpits mingling with the lingering aroma of her shampoo – honey, jasmine, and rose.

Close to midnight, there's a message from Kieran.

Sorry. I hid my phone at home in my room. I was at the club with Rachel. I went out on the spur of the moment, as I needed

to dance. She knew why and was supportive. She' was good to be with tonight.

Marianne checks her phone at two a.m. After reading Kieran's text, she's pissed off and can't sleep. He's at it, *again:* amassing women to soothe and support him. Is he blind to the fact it's not acceptable, even more so now she's slept with him? It's not as though he was the only boy brought up in a family of girls. There's being comfortable in a woman's company, and then there's ...

Before Marianne has time to respond in the morning, there's a text from him.

Does a girl want to meet a guy for a coffee?

She sure does! She's over the 'open up' and the 'pull back'. She rings him.

He's shocked but not scared off when she tells him how she feels.

"Marianne, it changes nothing between us. I'm grateful you've put me a little more in touch with your needs. I'm sorry. I didn't do it intentionally. My feelings have been shut down for so long; sometimes, I have trouble moderating my actions. I can see now that I didn't consider your feelings. Thank you for not getting angry and having the courage to express what you feel."

"You're a puppy that's desperate for a tummy rub from anyone willing to give one. If what we have continues to develop, I believe we can attain a lasting bond. Time will tell. But I can't stand on shifting ground forever."

"I'm unpredictable at times because when my emotions take over my good sense it terrifies me. You are much more than a friend to me. You always make me feel safe and secure, and my aim is to ensure you feel that way, too."

Then he says the words she's been waiting to hear for months.

"Bottom line is, I have fallen for you. I will always treat you with the utmost respect. You are precious to me."

Marianne has a Toyota feeling moment. It's worthy of a new rock 'n' roll move. The Trampoline.

The next text message Kieran sends Marianne has six hearts in different colours.

When Ana returns on Sunday night, it's a 'we need to talk', and Marianne knows she's in for an earful.

"You know I disagree with you and Kieran being together; yet, when I ask you to look after my place, you use it as a love nest. You're—" A sharp look cuts her off.

"Stop there, Ana. Who's been gossiping?"

"No one. Janet in the villa next door commented on what a lovely looking couple you were. The details came out from there."

"Does she know Renata?"

"For fuck's sake, Marianne. That's not the point. You're both doing the wrong thing. While he is still in the same house as his wife, he is cheating on her. What are you going to do when your little bubble bursts? If you allow this triangle, neither of you has any respect for yourselves or your spouses. You're certainly showing me no respect either. You aren't to be together in my place when I'm away."

The exchange ends with Marianne saying, "I'm not letting you control what I do and don't do. Perhaps you should find someone else to look after Houdini when you're away, or take him with you to Grant's place."

The friendship is chipped but not broken. Marianne and Ana have been friends too long for that. Mending bridges will have to wait till they go to the next dance fest at Nerangi in May; unless either has a life drama that needs a friendly ear.

The conversation, however, leaves its mark. An inherent truth nags at Marianne. She unloads on Kieran.

"I am sorry you are wearing all her angst, Marianne. It's certainly not pleasant."

"She said that if you could easily do it to your wife of almost thirty years, you could do it to me as well, and that I need to wake up to myself."

"We both know what I deal with in my marriage. Ana doesn't. A relationship between us would be totally different."

"She also said that you have left it so long already – years – that she doesn't believe you will leave your wife while you can have me on the side, and that you must have no respect for me either. She really stuck the knife in."

"I think you know I have the utmost respect for you, and I don't believe you are merely a friend with benefits. I care mountains for you."

All the uncertainty plays with Marianne's head. She's a woman under a streetlamp looking for clarity in the shadows. She's dissecting every word. "I don't believe' – a poor choice of words or an out? What the hell does 'I care mountains' mean? Maybe instead of spy stories about intrigue and espionage, he should brush up on mistakes men make that destroy a relationship.

That night she sends him a text.

A man must take care of his woman, and a woman must take care of her man. No one is before the other. It's about teamwork. Goodnight, sweet man xoxoxo

There's no reply. Marianne sends it again.

Goodnight, beautiful lady. xx

She already knows the only teamwork Kieran is focusing on now is his training for the Dragon Boat National Championship at Getaway Lakes, Dongarra. Five days, Wednesday to Sunday, in late April.

Marianne is relieved that the demands of his training will give her some breathing space to get her head together.

Puppet on a String

It's now two months since Kieran and Marianne began dating and three days since he's made love to her. He has yet to tell his wife he and Marianne are an item.

Marianne has been more than patient. Stupid, Ana would say for sure. Well, Ana, Little Misadventure is drawing a line in the sand. She will not be Kieran's little secret anymore. Will he even start the road to settlement and divorce? Will it ever be just them?

Conflict starts in Marianne's relationship with Kieran due to problems Renata causes. Although his wife has told him she has no feelings for him – 'repulsed' was the word she used – now she's saying she loves him, that the marriage is fine. Other times, that she loves him but is not *in love* with him. Her mind games have become two for the price of one: Marianne is collateral damage. Surely, indifference, not outrage, means no feelings. Indifferent, his wife is not! She always wants to know what he's doing. She has her spies. He's a puppet on a string.

Before Kieran leaves for the Nationals, he and Marianne meet for an evening meal at the Memari Thai Restaurant. During dinner Marianne voices the question that's been sizzling in her brain for weeks. "Why don't you leave?" Her kind tone takes the edge off the words.

He's heard something similar before from his mates, not a question but an imperative. 'You need to leave her, Kieran. It's disgusting the way she treats you.'

"I don't want to lose the home I designed and built." As he says it, he visualises his hilltop home set back from the coastline, the floor to ceiling glass and the expanse of ocean. Then there's all the capital – monetary and human – that created this Pacific paradise: huge loans; the handful of mortgage switches to ensure a better deal; refinancing for upgrades; the years spent laddering, hammering, painting, maintaining. Each a small smooth patient step forward to win the property race.

Marianne gets it, but is it possible, just possible, that Kieran still loves his wife. When he walks her to her car, the held question spills.

"Do you still love her?"

His response hits her in the stomach with the impact of a sixteen-kilo kettlebell training weight. It's honest and brutal.

"Yes, but it's not reciprocated, and you and I are together."

Suddenly, her mouth is dry, her fingers cold. Unblinking, she presses her lips together hard, her entire innards quiver, her limbs tremble, her heart cleaves. *Fuck. Fuckity. Fuck. Fuck. Fuck.* The anger and hurt stinging her now will turn inwards to depression. She can't afford to go there. "That does it! I've had enough. Just leave. I can't be the third person here. If you want to be with me, you need to finish it with her. I've had enough of wait and see."

"I'm sorry." He tries to hold her gaze, but his eyes sink to the pavement. He turns and walks away. Poor Mara Mia. Poor Mister Fuck-Up. He wants to turn around. Explain. Plead. But he cannot dredge up the action or the words.

As Marianne closes her car door, she bursts into tears. She is drowning in all of this. Is she being used? Does he genuinely love her? She wants to crawl into a hole and hide as much as she wants to run after him, as much as she wants him to turn around – explain, reassure, hold her close.

With a face covered in tears and snot, she drives to Ana's place. Ana opens the door, gives Marianne a tight bear hug and squirrels away the I-told-you-so.

"How can he possibly still love his wife when she treats him like shit? She doesn't touch him in any way, not even a kiss on the cheek to say goodbye. He's living in a mistake that needs white-out."

"Despite the facts showing otherwise, Kieran is stuck in a fiction that isn't the reality. He believes, underneath it all, his wife is still the woman he first married. He's blind to the reality of who Renata has become. We all have our blind beliefs even when reality punches us in the face with the truth. That's how it was with my fixation on Dan."

"I know he said he always thought he wasn't good enough for Renata. I guess that fact alone makes him blame himself for the failure of his marriage. As far as I can make out, over time his gentleness brought out the bully in her."

Kieran doesn't ring or text Marianne. On Tuesday after work, he heads up north for the State Championships; it's all he'll focus on for the next five days. The best paddlers in the country will be there, much younger than his team. Mentally he is tired and stressed.

How he misses the regular weekend men's camps that over the years restored his energy and de-stressed him. Four-wheel drives and bottomless cans of beer. Sun-down, dinner finished, 'Circle of Wisdom' around the campfire, and blokey things such as the best way to tie a mattress to the top of a car. Even back then, the others at the camp had witnessed the slow corrosion of his confidence: him having to second guess every aspect of himself.

Around a campfire, the flickering warmth invited relaxation, and the clear expanse of star-studded sky was an invitation to ponder personal matters alongside the ways of the world. The *real* stuff. Not to say that you didn't get the hilarious harmless practical jokes, too – it was a given. Once it started, everyone was on a roll. There was the 'lock-someone-in-their-tent' prank with a paper clip placed over the top of the zipper track; best if it allowed the prank target to open the tent a little bit before the paper clip did its work. In the morning there'd be a, "*Help*, my tent zipper's stuck!"

"Did you hear anything, Kieran?"

"No, mate. Must be the wind."

"Funny, Steve's either not up yet, or he's gone walkabout."

An even louder plea for help. "Dead set, I know you can hear me. Let me out, you pair of drongos. Stop larrikin' about."

"Reckon he must still be in his tent. Go and check on him, would you, Kieran."

"No worries. Okay, Steve ... coming. No need to go off like a frog in a sock."

Then there was the 'shake up the beer can in the esky' prank. Wait and see who gets it – *hello, volcano*! The best classic ever was a couple of thin cojoined uncooked sausages wrapped in clingwrap at the bottom of a sleeping bag. You get the idea. Men being boys.

After these weekends away, Kieran would return home content and emotionally super-fit. Within days, Renata would bring him down. Even at breakfast, she'd be on the hunt as she stabbed at the butter and slathered it over her toast. There was the time she hurled two knives in the sink. The harsh clatter of steel on steel.

"The knives are smeary."

"Okay, I missed two. I'm sorry. You don't do a perfect job all the time yourself."

He didn't have time to get out the, 'Please stop hounding me.' she knew was coming.

She'd picked up the small plastic benchtop composting bin and emptied it on the floor.

"See if you can do a better job with that."

Even now, the 'how' and 'why' of her continuing antagonism remain late-night thoughts that rack him notch by notch.

On Wednesday morning at Getaway Lakes, the water is a calm cup of milky tea due to the cloudy sky. Four days of predicted sunshine will end up a mixture of drizzle and driving rain with occasional clear patches.

There's a fair amount of brainwork being a sweep. The safety of the crew is in Kieran's hands. Decisions must be swift and correct. He's enjoying the challenge of Wednesday's training day before the Masters racing days on Thursday and Friday.

On the third morning at eight forty-five – State versus State Racing Day – Kieran charges his team headlong down the course. Fifty metres to go and heading for a silver medal. *Disaster.* Another boat overtakes too close, and the wake catches the back of his boat. Despite his yell, "*Stop the boat!*" he can't avert the disaster. The boat tips over under full power, rolling and throwing paddlers, caps, shoes and paddles everywhere – dignity overboard. They are bailed out and towed to shore. There's no call Kieran could have made to avert the disaster. The heat is over in 2.06.30 (2 minutes and 6.3 seconds) for the winners. The nose of the dragon's head pipping the closest rival by a couple of seconds.

Kieran remains consumed by the mess he's made of things with Marianne, out of his comfort zone in more ways than one. He misses her, but it's also a bitter-sweet relief not to be caught between two women. He does not text Marianne. He does not call her. What's he going to say anyway? Whatever he said would sound pathetic. He's a man utterly alone again, without the touch, trust and affection of a woman.

Days pass. Marianne waits, hoping that Kieran will ring begging her to come back. He is due back Sunday, as he didn't plan to stay for the junior and premier racing days.

Monday. Tuesday.

Nothing.

She begins to realise the depth of how impossible it is for him to unleash himself from behaviours and beliefs that no longer serve him. He's handcuffed by passivity and duct-taped with fear. If she wants him, she'll have to make a move to a way back to where they were. He does the best he can. He's deluged, defeated, desolate. Who is she to judge? What's the cure for trauma and abuse? Unconditional acceptance. Focus on where you want to be, Marianne, not on where you are now.

Alone and fragile – her husband has boxed up his belongings, ready to move out of the marital home – Marianne texts Kieran when she still hasn't heard from him by Wednesday. *Would a friend help a girl to look at a villa?*

Within seconds there's a response from Kieran. *Sure. Happy to help. I know how difficult these decisions are on your own.*

She sends him a thumbs-up emoji.

He smiles to himself and texts back, *I forgot to mention my fee. It could be astronomical but not unaffordable for a resourceful lady such as you.*

I could pay you via some hot lovin', would that be sufficient?

More than. He can't resist adding, *as long as you're in that little red dress and high heels.*

Wow, the way she looked that night at Langaratta – so gorgeous. Her smile and the closeness of her had blown him away. His 'Lady in Red'. What a fool. Remember, Kieran, tell her next time, and don't just stand there staring with your mouth half-open.

On Friday morning, he sends her a text. *Hi, this is Kieran's taxi service. Would you care to make a reservation for a private car and attentive driver for this evening's do? Your loving man.*

Hi, my sweet man. Cinderella awaits.

His pretty woman is back!

On an early June weekend, Kieran and Marianne drive north to a beach house at Sandy Cape, a cornucopia of beautiful beaches. Binaro town centre is only a ten-minute drive and is home to Leviathan Lakes Shopping Centre with all its discount stores.

Kieran surprises her; he's moved out of the marital home into the investment unit he and Renata own. He hopes Marianne doesn't ask, "Why now?" It's an answer she won't want to hear; she'll end up hating him, just like Renata. He's so exhausted; he's heading for an emotional crash. He's caught in the middle of the excessive push and pull of two women. It's taking its toll. Better to choose happy over hollow.

"How did it go?"

A 'how' not a 'why'. A wave of relief flushes over Kieran.

"There was a huge exhausting night of talking, but no violence or yelling. Mind you, I slept better. I think it's finally sinking in about a settlement; she seems more accepting. This morning before I left was not one of those coffee and conflict mornings. Just pleasantries."

Marianne says nothing. Has his wife regrouped with pleasantries in preparation for a major assault, or has the game plan truly changed?

Marianne is sure that Renata will spin the lie that Kieran left her for 'that rock 'n' roll woman'. The truth is she'd asked him for a divorce six months before Marianne's relationship with Kieran began.

On Saturday after a beach walk and breakfast, Kieran shares his morning plan.

"How about I drive you to the shopping centre for a few hours. I'll wait around, and you can duck and dive into any shop you want without me dragging my heels?"

"You'd do that?"

"Sure. I know women just love to shop, especially for a bargain."

After an hour and forty-five, he rings her. She knows he must be getting antsy. She's just on her way back to their rendezvous point with one brown bag – La Perla lingerie, *50% Off.*

"So, what's in the bag?"

"That's for you to find out after our night of dancing tonight."

Their weekends away are how together should be – new people, new places. They transfuse each other with a depth of freedom, a depth of loving.

Astrologically, Marianne is a fire sign and Kieran, air. They fuel one another – energetic, hot, expressive.

Around the Bend

Summer is long gone. It's June. The first month of winter. The nights are becoming darker and colder – twelve degrees. Backed into a corner, Marianne intends to bring summer's twenty-two-degree warmth and sunlight back into her life. Time for her to turn the corner and change direction, she as driver and Kieran as passenger.

She suggests they go away for two nights. Brume. A sleepy coastal retreat at its barefoot best. Beaches and a beautiful bush setting. Kieran is keen on a weekend getaway, as he needs a breather.

They pay fifty-fifty to book a quaint B&B with late 1880s origins. Located in a former lighthouse keeper's cottage, it sits atop a large hillock overlooking the ocean, embraced by a mountain range and enlivened by heavy gales.

The white rendered, white picket fence building has interiors in accents of blue. The décor is modern-classic, comfortable and super relaxing. No pancake pillows here! There is a king-size bed, and a free-standing bath looks out from a sizeable window with unmatched views of the blue ocean and the purple-haze of a mountain as far as the eye can see.

The owners, Steve and Gayle, don't live on the premises. They have left a basket full of fruit, all the things for a cooked breakfast and, most importantly of all, a Grant Burge Fifth Generation Barossa Merlot 2016.

The bed doona is a lightly toasted white marshmallow, and Marianne can see the cord for an electric blanket. Kieran is in his element, as there's a wood heater and a stack of firewood in the small living room; the opportunity to light a fire. He so loves the days when autumn falls into winter.

Within minutes two happy souls lounge in front of a blazing fire and watch the firelight flicker across the bulbs of their long-stemmed glasses. The merlot is soft and silky on the palate. When Marianne leans into Kieran, she can smell the red wine's aroma of cherries, dark plum and spices on his breath. Outside, the sky is clear and studded with stars.

Smiles, laughter, touch and warmth animate the room. Kieran is happy, energised, truly alive. The drizzle of depression has left him. Marianne. She's breathed new life into him. With her, he feels so different – a real person. Not lonely, not lost – loved. She's become the reason he can look forward to each day.

Before bed they take a bath; the lavender bubble bath is another thoughtful gesture by their hosts. Kieran lowers himself into the aromatic mist first and stretches out. Marianne slips her body between his legs and leans with her back against his chest. Her upper chest and breasts are out of the warmth, so Kieran takes a face washer and dips it into the steamy water and lays its soaking heat over her chilled skin.

Marianne melts each time his hands arrange the weighted warmth over her. She leans back into him.

As they chit-chat, they fill in the gaps about each other and discover they both married at nineteen and are twice married. Their relationship is a 'third chance romance' for Marianne, but a 'fourth chance romance' for Kieran; he had a nine-year de facto relationship between his two marriages.

"Tell me something about yourself I would never guess?"

"Are you suggesting I have skeletons in my closet, Mara Mia?"

"Come on. I'm serious."

"Well, I used to play A-Grade soccer, was a championship ballroom dancer in my teens and played banjo in a band in my twenties."

"*Show-off.* There is no 's' on the end of *something.* Your answer sounds more like 'Truth or Lie'."

'I did say a ballroom dancer, *not a* ballerina."

"That's a relief! Skeletons in a closet I can come to terms with, but you'd be pushing it with a tutu."

He grins. "Your turn."

"I was a child model when I was five. In the David Jones catalogues."

"There you go – destiny. Doesn't the top soccer player always end up with a model?"

"Know-it-all!" and she flips onto her front. The warm wet surge of her breasts contour over his chest and his battered soul. As she kisses him passionately on the lips, she feels his penis and testicles float between her inner thighs. Just as quickly, she flips back to the way she was.

Kieran sings his own adaptation of Frankie Valli's 1967 biggest solo hit, 'Can't Take My Eyes Off You', in a rich baritone voice. "You're just a bathtub flirt. I'm sending out an alert. You know I'm all eyes for you, and my heart's all askew. I wanna …"

She lobs the dripping washer at him. He's just so funny and adorable when he's completely relaxed.

As they float, Kieran ripples the warm water over her. She feels his breath in her ear and the relaxation in his voice when he tells her, "I feel very comfortable and at ease with you, so there may be lots of outpouring on information from me about feelings."

"My darlin', darlin' man, that's exactly how I want it to be for you. I want you to know that I have longed to have a partner such as you. Someone I can be open with about anything and everything. I feel so fortunate. I want to be there to help you heal and repair the broken parts of your heart and soul. You can trust me and rely on me to be there for you. I love you dearly."

"I have strong feelings for you, Marianne and will be your rock whenever you need me. It's important to me that you know that."

They haven't drunk enough for it to be the wine talking. It's the intimacy that time and trust bring. As Kieran and Marianne snuggle in bed, the westerly blast of the strong winds and pounding of the king tide remind them they are safe and together. Marianne loves the warmth of his bare flesh against hers. He's a good one. Lucky. That's what she is. Keep hold of this one, Marianne.

Late on the Saturday morning, when Marianne opens the door, it frames a kangaroo on the front lawn as if posed for a Centrefold photo shoot for *National Geographic's* 'Pet of the Month'. It's on its side, its front legs under its shoulders, and its hind legs and tail outstretched at a languid twenty degrees.

The following morning as Kieran stands outside, coffee mug in hand, Marianne takes a photo of his hand in the foreground, beyond which three wallabies stand equidistant from one another in a hear no evil, see no evil, taste no evil pose.

Immediately afterwards, she glides back inside the cottage, puts her phone down and grabs the bag of feed the owners have left for the wallabies. Outside, she places the grains on the flat of her palm, extends her arm and waits. *Oh, my god!* The sheer gentleness of it. So unexpected. Soft, delicate paws finely circle her wrist, and a 240-grit sandpaper tongue tickles the tiny grains from her palm. Marianne is so in the moment that she doesn't notice Kieran watching her and smiling. Love has become the way he looks at her.

When they go for their early afternoon walk hand in hand, buffeting air and salt spray cleanse their lungs and rouge their cheeks. Dolphins pass by at the base of the large lighthouse, and the charismatic head of a humpback corkscrews up out of the ocean.

The beach is a place of granite boulders and rusted wrecks, either twenty fathoms deep or dune buried. Marianne sure wishes Kieran would leave the sinking ship of his marriage. Slow and steady as you go, Marianne. In the moment, he is fine. Out of it, he shrinks. So full of fear. Any decision made will be by her gentle force.

When Marianne returns on Sunday night, Adam does not ask about her weekend. Likewise, she tells him nothing. He has accepted that what his soon-to-be ex-wife does now is her business, not his. In a few weeks, he knows she'll be away for a whole week dancing and, when she returns, she'll be a single woman starting a new life in her villa. He'll be a single man in a holiday rental till he sorts out where he'll be.

Just before seven that night, there's a text message alert on Marianne's phone. She opens it.

I hope that sometime in the future we will head off on a proper holiday together.

Kieran's phone chirps a few seconds later.

Me, too. I just loved our time alone. I felt it would make or break us. I am happy to say that it has just made our relationship even more substantial.

Then there's a ping-pong of exchanges.

Do you reckon we'll manage a few weeks away together, Marianne?

Hope so. I know it will be beautiful and memorable. Mind you, if we drink all the alcohol, we may not remember a thing.

Don't worry, you can drink, and I can drive, and I'll do all the remembering for the two of us.

It figures he'd say that. He's such a sweetheart. *You do know you make my heart flutter every time you say something nice?*

You are a darling woman, and the nice stuff comes easy with you because I appreciate who you are.

When Marianne unpacks her case from the weekend away, she discovers she's packed Kieran's phone charger by mistake. When Kieran unpacks his, he finds the earring Marianne thought she'd lost.

Heads, I'm yours. Tails, you're mine.

Back at the unit, Kieran is unable to forget the weekend. He resists sending a late-night text to her because he knows she needs her sleep. Falling asleep at ten-thirty, phone in hand, he wishes it was *her* in his hands. He sends a text in the morning before work and ends it with two hearts and two smilies. It sums up their weekend away perfectly.

Monday, and in medical receptionist mode, Marianne texts Kieran in her break to ask if he's managed to get a doctor's appointment. She's concerned that he makes sure there's no blockage stopping blood flow to his penis.

Kieran's reply is instant. *I'll get onto it in a couple of weeks. No rush.*

Marianne knows from work that two weeks is always the time a person gives when they have no intention of doing something. Two weeks takes the heat off temporarily, as the asker believes the askee will do it, and it is a long enough time for the asker to forget about it. No one gets away with that with Marianne. Kieran will need to learn that. He so obsessively weighs up the pros and cons of every decision; consequently, his indecision makes things a big deal when they are not a matter of life and death.

If Kieran was in front of her, he would fold his arms and say, "Let's close the topic of conversation."

Within minutes she texts him. *You know me, hun. No wait and see. I know the girl on the booking service. I got you an appointment for ten a.m. this Friday with the specialist. You need to prioritise this for yourself and for me – for us.*

His inflexible, avoidant self knows she's right. That girl certainly has his back.

Thank you. I love your organisational skills, my beautiful angel eyes. xxoo 😊

See you later, Mister Pro-cras-ti-na-tor. 😉

Baby Come Back

In August Marianne and Kieran book tickets for the 2018 Tamworth Country Music Festival. The late January festival will be huge: seven hundred artists across one hundred and twenty venues. She and Kieran will never make it. Marianne will be forced to on-sell their tickets.

For Marianne, the two prior months have been moving and unpacking boxes. For Kieran, it's been poor sleep and waking at four in the morning, his mind a replay of scenes from his marriage. The last of the boxes unpacked and the contents rehomed, Marianne wakes on Friday morning drained and exhausted. A hacking cough and a pain in her kidneys have kept her awake most of the night. She rings in sick to work, medicates herself and spends the day in bed.

On Saturday morning, Kieran checks on her by text. *Good morning, darling. How is my cute receptionist today? Chilly morning! I miss your cuddles and can't wait to wrap my arms around you. See you at your villa tonight. I will prepare a meal.*

Thank you, my darlin' man. Tablets have not kicked in yet. Still in bed. Hardly any voice. How are you this morning? xxoo

I'm fine. Real estate agent, then a catch-up. xxoo

He doesn't mention his nightmare from last night that lingers as mild panic in his chest; a disastrous dragon boat start at a competition. The first stroke of the start is explosive and, warmed up, the first three to ten strokes are the most solid ever. Then it happens. A quick twist of his shoulder, a "Stop the boat!" The limp of the boat back to shore – disqualified. No row, row, row your boat for months, as in the dream the outcome is a rotator cuff injury.

After he picks up paperwork for the investment unit from the real estate agent, he meets a friend for Saturday brunch.

"How's it going, Action Man?"

"Bored out of my brain in the unit, Ross. With no house or lawn and garden to maintain, I'm less Action Man and more Mister Potato Head." He doesn't add that he has no energy or motivation; fear, boredom, and loneliness percolate throughout his day. He certainly doesn't mention the nightmare he had last night. Their conversation steers to State of Origin footie, the Soccer World Cup, music and how the kids are doing. Kieran has all the sporting details, as that's all he's watched on the television.

As he leaves, there's an alert on his phone, an incoming text message. Once he's read it, he texts Marianne. *Sorry, darling. Dragon boat text. Need sweep for tonight. No one else is available. See you at six-thirty. I'll pick up dinner for us.*

Over the weekend, Marianne's symptoms deepen into bronchial asthma. Acute exacerbation – heavy duty antibiotics. Unable to speak, she can only wheeze. At times in the night, she struggles to breathe as she gasps for air and her chest tightens with intense suffocating pressure. As fear and anxiety kick in, her heart races, and she begins to hyperventilate. Lightheaded, she reaches for the paper bag in the bedside drawer, breathes slowly into it until her breathing slows and flows up from her belly rather than high in her chest.

She knows why she's unable to breathe. There's no clear-cut way forward in her relationship with Kieran. She's trapped in no man's land. Kieran has left the marital home; yet, marital yesterdays continue to ensnare him. Marianne is so close but, at the same time, so far away from what she wants. Why, oh why, does he continue to stand in his own way, allow Renata to bombard him with text messages all weekend?

Unsettled and on edge as the weekend draws to a close, Marianne's lungs continue to struggle to gain the respite of easy breaths. She texts Kieran to apologise. *I am so sorry for last night. Sick for so long – my spirit is low. Find it hard to cope with everything when I feel like this. You're a beautiful man, and I value you so much. I don't want to lose you. I need another couple of days to try to get on top of this. xx*

As tears prick her eyes, her phone pings.

I'm still here for you. Take all the time you need to get better. I'll still be here.

That's not how it feels to her. He's neither here nor there. Or is it, there and never here?

He's all over the damn place.

Two days later, when Kieran starts going downhill too – headache, rough throat, a worsening cough – Marianne is finally on the mend. Welcome relief!

Hi, hun. Sending you lots of 🌺🌺🌺🌺🌺

I want to be the reason you look down at your phone and smile, then walk into a pole.

I look forward to collecting your 🗓️🗓️🗓️🗓️🗓️

He's taking cold and flu tablets, a cough suppressant, throat lozenges and long beach walks. The demands on his attention are lightweight when he walks – side-stepping the pebbles, the wheel of an eagle, the brief hellos – and allow him to let go of the dread that tries to trip him.

At eight in the morning, on the second Tuesday in August, Kieran sends Marianne a card capture photo – *Happy Birthday!*

Thank you! With you, I've found the perfect partner, the best friend, and the sweetest love anyone has ever known. And I am so grateful life led me to you.

For a month from early August to September, Kieran stays over at the villa from two to six nights a week. He feels so alone in the unit on his own.

Six months later, conflict seeps into their relationship: Renata's machinations and Kieran's inability to know how to deal with them. Renata, having played the blame game, is now telling him that she still loves him, that the marriage is fine as far as she is concerned. The result? Kieran's mired in the quicksand of emotional confusion and infused with pangs of guilt that only the conscientious and scrupulous have.

Marianne has an appointment with a psychologist. She comes away from it with a prescription for Pristique – she'd rather not – and, 'you have the power to choose what you accept and what you let go of … he doesn't need to pretend the damage never happened. Healing means it no longer controls our lives.' It's time to handle things her way, to honour herself.

Toeing Kieran's line has gone on for too long. It's become destructive to her health. Then, as if things weren't bad enough, there's the seismic shock of an entry in his notebook.

It's a Saturday, and Kieran's at early morning training. He's left in a rush, his morning cuppa half-finished, the cup unwashed.

His notebook lies on the coffee table with a pen snuggled between the pages. Of course, Marianne is going to flick through it.

There's just the everyday stuff till she comes to a late June entry written four months into their relationship: the same time he was telling Marianne how he felt about her. It's written in his sizeable bold hand with its slight left slant and significant gaps between the words. Some letters of the words joined, others not. Every word sits exactly on the line, the dot of each 'i' precisely above. At the end of words, the inflated loops of the y's parachute collide and tangle with part of the word on the line below.

> I love Renata and will do so forever. She leaves me weak at the knees. She's beautiful. I loved the feeling of her legs intertwined with mine, the smell of her skin and hair. I wanted to grow old with this woman.

Gutted, Marianne is catatonic. Warmth drains from her body. She seeks the sanctuary of the spare bed and curls into a foetal position. Numb, she can neither sob nor scream. Broken, used, washed-up is what she is. At this moment, she *hates* him. She wants to spit, stamp, tear him to shreds.

No wonder Kieran had said to her that if she ever spoke to Renata, she'd end up hating him. He was forever telling Marianne not to worry about things, as Renata and he would never get back together. How could Kieran not see this woman for what she was, what he was allowing her to do to him with the acid drip of her abuse? No wonder when the two of them were sorting out their settlement, he sometimes cancelled plans with Marianne, caught up with Renata for lunch or dinner, was always at the beck and call of her text messages.

Drained, Marianne falls asleep. She wakes surrounded by the fading light of early evening. Angry and depressed, she rings Ana. As soon as she hears Ana's voice on the other end, she bursts out crying. Ana lets her sob till she can make sense of what's happened.

"Marianne, what can I say. I am sorry to hear you're so distressed, but rarely does any good come of reading other people's innermost thoughts. Take a deep breath, blow your nose. Then, pour yourself a glass of wine and curl up on the lounge. I'll do the same. I'll ring you back in five."

Ana does as she promises. "Feeling a little better?"

"Sort of."

"Marianne, when you asked Kieran outright a month or so before this entry, he admitted he still loved his wife."

"You're right. I know that. But it still cuts deep."

"I know. It's tough to see Kieran's feelings on the page. Look, Marianne, I know Kieran hasn't turned out to be a one-trick pony. I was very wrong about that. But you need to understand many men find emotional adjustment challenging. He and you were coming from totally different places. You were over Adam, ready to move on. Kieran was conflicted. You brought joy into his life, but he still loved his wife. Can you let go of what was written for his eyes only?"

"I guess so. We are just so good together, and that wife of his is some piece of work."

"You *are* great together, but you have to remember, suddenly the poor guy was in a serious relationship with you before he had time to process things, to find out who he was outside his marriage. Does that make sense?"

"Yes."

"How are you feeling about things now?"

"Better for a good friend and a glass of cheap red. Thanks, Ana."

"So, what are you going to do to cheer yourself up, besides more wine?"

"I'm just so drained. I'm going back to bed. I have a hairdresser's appointment tomorrow and a manicure so that's good. Thanks for being there."

"That's okay. Sleep well. I'll check on you in the morning. See that you're okay."

"Thanks, Ana."

Marianne says nothing to Kieran about the diary entry for the simple reason that Ana is correct; however, her body is unable to digest and eliminate the bitter peel of the words. She's sick again. More antibiotics, a chest x-ray. A week off work.

Kieran is having trouble with his lower back. Marianne thinks of the idiom 'to have no backbone', no stable sense of stability to allow him to face challenges. The way things are cannot continue. She *must* deal with what Kieran has neglected. She wants him, but she does not want his unresolved baggage invading their territory. The balance between taking and giving is out of whack.

"Kieran, you cannot go through life avoiding what is difficult. You need to tell Renata we are together."

"Marianne, I can't do this now. I've had enough of that subject. You need to let it go."

He may as well have said, "Shut up, don't speak up."

She can't remain caught in this looping track of pause and replay. "Kieran, if you won't tell her, I will. I've let it go on for far too long. No more!"

"Please don't do that. I don't want you speaking to Renata. It'll make things worse. I know where you are coming from, but you've got to realise I have a lot to sort out. I need to do it properly, including telling Renata, in *my* time, when the timing is right,"

"Well, the time may never be right. Time is precious. You never know what might happen in a week, a month, a year. And, what about *my* time? I need you to commit to our relationship. If not, there's no chance of this going any further. One of us needs to deal with this, *now*."

"Do *not* go near her. You have no idea what she's capable of. She'd eat you up for breakfast." He turns and walks away to water the plants in the garden.

Eat Marianne for breakfast? *No way*. Marianne is more than capable of giving as good as she gets. She would annihilate Renata, for sure, and it's got nothing to do with her Marianne's powerful left hook honed by her boxing training at the gym. But no, she won't go there, as it would jeopardise her relationship with Kieran. He would not like her at all. So, yet again, she and Kieran are in the gone place. Togetherness. Gone. Laughter. Gone. The time of truly being themselves. Gone. Gone. Gone.

Apart from Ana, no one knows of the swerves and reversals. At their most recent weekend at Langaratta, when she and Kieran were walking back to their hotel, arm in arm amongst the others, Rachel had remarked, "You look so good together. There's good energy between the two of you. Have you ever disagreed?"

"No, not really. We've had issues with the toilet roll and the toothpaste tube. I got stuck into him."

Kieran nodded and smiled in agreement.

"After I'd finished getting stuck into him, he said, 'Is that all you've got?' I smiled and said, 'Yes, it is.' And that was the end of that."

"I bet I can guarantee what the issue was. Which way do you roll? Which way do you squeeze?"

"Too right. It really annoys me when I put the toilet paper free side out, and Kieran insists on changing it to the wall side. I think it's a man thing or the Scottish in him. Wall side, I can only ever get one sheet out before it seizes up. Not enough to dry a tear, never mind wipe a bottom."

"Annoying. You want annoying. Marianne thinks the toothpaste tube is an invitation to freeform squeezing. I am a squeeze from the bottom and cut the tube, man. I can service my teeth for an extra fortnight out of a tube Marianne discards."

"I bet with the toilet paper, you're a folder, and Marianne is a scruncher."

The two of them leant into each other and laughed. Kieran's smile. It was the smile of a man who, for the first time in years, felt seen, heard, and valued: able to derive sustenance from a relationship.

Rachel. Marianne really welcomes her company. She's so easy going and, whilst she has a filter, you wouldn't want to strain your coffee through it. She has the New Age hippy vibe.

The unit at Bellows Beach is rented out, so in early September Kieran moves to Lilly Pilly Falls into a granny flat owned by a friend of Renata's. It's a twenty-minute drive from Marianne's villa. Why on earth did he agree to that? Marianne knows why – it was easy.

Marianne resolves to contact Renata.

"I've sent a message to Renata letting her know we have been in a relationship since February."

He's caught in the trap of a pragmatic white lie; he told Renata that it was May. It was as much a truth as it was a lie. It was the month he'd moved out of the marital home and after he and Marianne had been intimate. Renata hadn't taken it well, and he'd further infuriated her by saying, "Why is this upsetting you so much? It's how we got together."

He'd dated Renata while he was in the dying throes of a nine-year de-facto relationship that had degraded to 'living separate lives, just financial' as he put it. It *always* niggled and nagged Renata that the pattern would repeat itself in their marriage. Yes, there's no doubt Marianne's text will bring down a tsunami of fury from his wife.

"You did that? Why?"

"Yes. I wanted her to know."

"What did you send?"

She shows him.

I have been seeing Kieran for seven months. Kieran told me your marriage was over when we met. Please let me know if you are trying to reconcile, and I will walk away and let you both sort out your marriage.

"I never heard back."

His phone pings with a stream of messages, "*Well,* I just have."

He's in the Badlands again.

He slumps in the chair. "Renata's furious. She's going to call the police. I told you to leave well alone." He's quietly furious with Marianne. His life at the moment is like paddling offbeat – a desynchronised chain of timing. "I have to go and sort this out."

It's an empty threat from Renata, but, overwhelmed, Kieran distances himself from Marianne for days turning into weeks. He is aware his feelings for his wife are unresolved. He can't cope with the pressure of Marianne harrying him for a premature commitment on an 'us' while he's still trying to resolve the conflict of a former 'we'. He's not even 'almost' divorced, and his son has wiped him. Flee man, flee.

Devastated, the story Marianne tells herself is that he doesn't care as much about their relationship as he did before. His greetings to her in texts become, 'Marianne'. No terms of endearment. Does he no longer see their relationship as a gift; a chance to grasp freedom and joy over fear? Trouble is change. He can't cope with either. Even though she lets him know she is there if he needs her, his underlying message is that he doesn't know what he wants or where's he's at.

He surprises Marianne with a visit, but only to tell her that he is not moving into the villa. Until the settlement is final, he needs to show Renata that they live separately. Kieran's decision pelts Marianne with the force of a micro blast storm. She holds herself together. Says nothing.

Nowadays, even the short loving humorous sayings Marianne texts – *If you're in your bed and I'm in mine, one of us is in the wrong place* – put Kieran on edge. He feels the prod.

Initially pessimistic and hesitant, she parks her wishful thinking and hopes. She digests what Kieran has said and starts to see why he's made the decision. She gets where he's coming from: he wants no complications before his settlement. She blows out her cheeks, grabs her phone and hits the speech bubble message icon. *Sorry for my initial response. I just expected you would be moving in with me. I shall stay focused on the bigger picture. I look forward to the day when we can both be free to enjoy our time together fully. You are an amazing man, and I consider myself so lucky to be in a relationship with you.*

His response? Well, what more could she expect? Other than,

Thank you for the heartfelt text.

Her response?

I am thankful to have you in my life.

What he types back adds to her depression.

No problem.

Okay! She knows he's struggling, emotionally unavailable, but it's difficult for her to shut and open her heart simultaneously. So, after days of dealing with her sense of rejection, she texts him. *Life is too short to live with regrets. So. Love the people who treat you right and forget about those who don't. Change is not always easy, but the payoff is worth it. Hang in there!*

There's an immediate ping.

I thought you might not be talking to me. I am sorry. My start today was terrible! My life at the moment is mind games and tears.

Hi, hun. You need to work this out as you go along. It's all part of your journey and getting to know yourself: your hopes, desires and what you can handle in life. We all have those cliff-like moments.

Thanks. I feel a bit broken. I'm trying to see where I am at. It's going to take time. Lilly Pilly Falls is comfortable, a refuge from things – dawn paddling. Sorry I've tangled you in my stuff. I'm a troubled soul. Frozen meals, footie and 'Home and Away' – boring.

As with Bridget Jones, Marianne is drowning her sorrows with, and into, a tub of Ben and Jerry's Vanilla Caramel Fudge ice cream. She's become the sad-lady-eating-all-the-ice-cream. After watching a Blu-ray of *Dirty Dancing*, she binge-watches taped episodes of *The Bachelorette* hosted by Sophie Monk. Who'd have guessed it? No one, except her and Ana. Everyone in the dancing group sees them as a perfect, perfect pairing. No idea both of them are unhappy. What the hell is happening? Has something changed between Kieran and his wife? Second thoughts? Does *he* still want to be with Renata if she's willing to take him back? Does *she* want to reconcile?

Kieran won't answer Marianne's questions. Always, 'Now isn't the right time.' Well, sometimes it isn't, but it's a polite out.

Avoidant. Emotionally dishonest. She pummels him with, "Am I right?" Eventually, he'll have to give her a straight answer.

During one phone call, Marianne lays her cards on the table. "Look, hun, I do want to be with you, but I hate living from day to day wondering if you are going to tell me you are sorry, as you've made a big mistake and want to be with Renata because it's so much easier financially. Please don't keep telling me you don't know what you want. If you want misery, then let me go, and I'll walk away."

At weekends Marianne is out dancing while he is home alone. She tells whoever asks, that Kieran is busy. It's a part-truth. The situation is embarrassing for them both, as others are so used to seeing them as an inseparable pair.

Three weeks into September, Marianne is not dancing because of nasty skin cancers on the back of her legs. She's popping basal cell carcinomas like popcorn. The specialist asks if she spent her youth belly down, reading books on the beach for hours. She looks at him as if he's psychic.

When Marianne tells Kieran about the carcinomas, he turns up at the villa with a beautiful bouquet of mulberry chrysanthemums in shades of purple, embraced by fern fronds. The flowers say what he can't say for himself at the moment.

Then, he's gone again – just texts.

Are you still dancing, Marianne?

I can't 'cos of the stitches. It's okay anyway 'cos the guy I want to dance with isn't there, so it doesn't really matter. 😢

He turns up at her door with more flowers.

"You must hate me?"

"No, I am angry with you, but I could never hate you. I am just sad about the disappearance of the fun times we've had during the eight months we've been together."

"The love?"

"I have not stopped loving you, Kieran."

"It doesn't seem that way."

"I just want to give you the space you need to sort your life out. I can't just sit around and put my life on hold while that happens. You need to understand that. When you're sorted, no second thoughts, if you still want an 'us', you have my number. Remember, the only person in charge of your life is you."

After he leaves, her thoughts take her back to their weekends at Langaratta, rocking 'n' a reeling and her favourite moves: the Cuddle Walk and the Carousel Twirl.

The Throwaway?

Well, that's another matter.

It's a complicated dance move, challenging for the man and the woman to execute seamlessly. It needs perfect timing, momentum and balance, and a male that leads his partner well. Kieran is an expert – a smooth, seamless spin. It's one of his favourite moves. His right hand to her right hand. A clockwise overhead spin. Then, his right hand around her waist in a quick smooth movement, into a whip-around while she's in a circular motion – no dead stop, no jerkiness. No, she didn't have to muddle through. He didn't make her look an incapable dancer; he accurately anticipated her arrival back to him and immediately initiated the backwards carousel.

Marianne loathed the feeling of being out of control, wantonly discarded to be picked up by Kieran at will and brought back. She discovered she was not the only woman who felt that way about that particular dance move. According to Rachel, most women are averse to the flick-and-let-go.

Marianne can't remember how long it took her to persuade Kieran to exclude that move from his repertoire.

"But that's one of my favourites."

"But, I dislike it. I'm asking you *not* to do that one."

Insistent, she sure was. "I told you *not* to do that." He got there eventually, or maybe she just got through eventually.

On the fourth Saturday in September, Kieran visits his sister and son in southwestern Melbourne. At seven in the evening, Marianne sends him a *Happy Birthday* before she leaves to go dancing with Rachel. He replies simply with, *Thanks*.

The rift between Kieran and his son is healing. They are in the pub having steak and chips.

"Max, I didn't want to involve you, and I didn't want to bad mouth your mum. I didn't want to lose you."

"Dad, I disagree with the way you did things. It would be best to have told Mum sooner and to have been more upfront about when the relationship began. I can't believe you did what you did. I've always trusted you."

"Sorry, I let you down, Max. I stuffed up."

Things are not going well for Kieran. The plan to sell the investment unit at Bellows Beach has fallen through because the tenant will not withdraw early from the lease. Like a bad throw in *Snakes and Ladders*, he's back at the beginning. He also feels he's letting Marianne down. He's shattered.

Her patience gone, Marianne is angry with him. How much longer can he keep pouring from an empty cup and not be ticked off? By repeating the cycle of being Mister Nice Guy to everyone, instead of assertive, confident and bold, he'll end up with what he's trying to avoid: more abuse and resentment from his wife. Marianne texts him. *Did Renata end up going to Melbourne?*

Not this weekend. She was here last weekend. No need to worry.

Now Marianne understands why there wasn't a barrage of texts the previous weekend.

I'm freezing down here. I am cuddling my pillow and missing my girl. I need to wrap my body around yours. I was up at seven for a six-kilometre beach walk at Sandy Hills and breakfast at the golf club. I had a lazy afternoon watching movies.

Good morning, darlin'. I am missing you too. I used your Trussardi Uomo shower gel last night so it would smell as if you were next to me as I slept.

City shopping today for raincoat and backpack. Melbourne prices – huge! City shopping is so overwhelming, even on a Monday. I think I've become a country boy. Lost my city slicker desire. I really only visit for my sister and Max. Back Tuesday. Usual late afternoon flight. May I drop in for dinner one night during the week?

Sounds as if you are not shopping fit. As for dinner, I will have to check my social calendar.

I'll sulk now but speak soon.

When he's back from Melbourne at five forty-five on Tuesday afternoon, he texts Marianne. *Missing you. May I drop in for a visit?*

You may.

There in fifteen … minutes, not days. 🌿

The next day it's, *Hi, Mara Mia, I would like to spend the evening with you if you want to see me. I so miss you.* 😘

Loving Yourself this Christmas

Mid-December marks ten months together. They've seen out all the year's seasons as a couple. It will be Kieran's first Christmas in thirty years without his family. He's still reeling over the fact that, over decades, someone's love can vanish. The betrayal by disconnection is gut-wrenching. He can't talk to Marianne about the future. He can't tell her he loves her anymore. He remains unable to break free from Renata.

Marianne is now hanging out for his settlement to go through. She sees this as the key to stability and security with him. Renata? She's one devious woman. As soon as she finds out Marianne and Kieran plan to go away to Langaratta dancing for a week in mid-December, she decides to go away at the same time. Kieran will have to look after their dog. Y*et again*, he's allowing Renata to call the shots. Marianne fumes with frustration and hurt. On Friday night she goes dancing without him.

As she's about to leave the villa there's a message from Kieran.
Have a good night.
Don't worry, I will.
OK. I'm not worried. I guess that I won't be missed.

You are always missed, but you made it clear that you didn't know what you would be doing. You'd just see how things worked out. I can't sit around waiting for you to make up your mind about what life you want. I refuse to sit around feeling sorry for myself.

Sorry, I'm just pissed off. I feel like crap, and I'm not much fun to be around. My emotions are all over the place. My head is playing games.

Yes, I can relate to that. Now you know how I feel.

Sorry again.

I wish you were here with me. I miss my dance partner. xx

Kieran's mood lifts with the sunny Saturday morning, a good paddle and morning tea with mates.

In the evening, it's the rock 'n' roll dance class Christmas party. Marianne is not going. She's a mess, can't handle another night of everyone asking where Kieran is, another night of putting on a happy face. Hide away is where she's at when all she wants to do is be with him. She's struggling to know what has gone wrong with them, *yet again*. They're spending less and less time together. She should have listened to Dan: 'If he cared about you, he would want to spend more time with you. It seems his wife is still his number one priority.'

She and Kieran are on the edge of breaking up with all that's going on. When they are together, Kieran's phone is a barrage of missed calls from Renata. Furious, frantic calls. 'Fuck-friend, fucking lying bastard.' Text messages saying that a married man should not have photos with another female. That he needs to get tested for HIV. As far as Marianne is concerned, the woman is a total bitch. Marianne knows what she'd delight in saying to her – it involves sex and travel. Also,

Renata's somehow accessed Marianne's Facebook page. She claims Marianne has posted that she and Kieran are engaged, and that the page had sixty-three comments.

"Her accusations have no foundation. She needs to show you proof. I never said we are engaged. You know we have no secrets, no lies between us. It is none of her business what I have on my Facebook page. If you were still in a relationship with her, I would not have posted photos of us. *All* our friends are aware we are together and are really happy for us, say we are well-matched. Unbeknown to them, they have no idea about the crap that goes on behind the scenes. *It needs to stop. I've had enough!*"

She shows him the 'See All Friends' on her account. She has ninety-one.

"You were never in doubt. Renata's not much good with technology. I did ask for proof. There was none. She's just confused."

The hell she is. "She's just causing trouble between us. How can you *not* see that? Until you take control of your life, things will never be different. Do you still love her?"

There's a pause. "Maybe."

Although the answer is as Marianne expects, when the man who said he loved her speaks it, the word stabs her heart with savage brutality.

"Just go, Kieran."

"I'm so sorry. Can I ask you to–"

"*No.* You can't ask me anything. *Go. Just go.*"

That night, while Marianne takes down their photos from her Facebook page, Kieran and his emotional mess fall asleep on top of his bed. The 'maybe' makes him sick to the stomach. He just wants his settlement to be over. Then, maybe then, things between him and Marianne will return to the way they were. Renata has him by the balls. She doesn't want him to have anything, not even his coin and stamp collection, and there's not a damn thing he can do about it. She's also changed the locks on the marital home.

Still all the way out at Lilly Pilly Falls, Marianne knows Kieran must be overwhelmed with loss – wife, son, home, dog, neighbours. On top of that, Christmas is close.

Worse is on a roll. Kieran's plans over Christmas are as reliable as ice cubes in a drink on a forty-degree day. First, Max is coming up. Then not, as Max is to fly his parents to Melbourne for Christmas. Then another backflip. Renata will go, and Kieran will stay to look after the dog.

Two days before Christmas, the Christmas plan firms. Max will fly up for a family Christmas. Kieran pops over to the villa to let Marianne know.

Marianne fully understands and supports Kieran if he wants to spend Christmas with his son. Max is still a tad offside, and Kieran needs to rebuild the bond when he has the chance.

"Kieran, you need to let Max know your side of the story. It's natural for a son to protect his mother, but it's a great disservice to you and to me, *not* to tell him."

Kieran looks at her, says nothing.

After he leaves, she lets his emotional and physical withdrawal sink in. She's a mix of acceptance and hurt. Kieran and Max, probably the only good thing that will come out of this Christmas. She can cancel the accommodation. They can book a weekend away another time. *But*, if it's *not* the *only* reason he's changing their plans at the very last minute, Marianne will feel that maybe she is not as crucial to Kieran as she thought.

Back at the granny flat, Kieran is on the patio having a cold one by himself when there's a text alert on his Samsung Galaxy.

When you find a king, keep him, when you find a queen, love and protect her. Don't reshuffle your cards because you might end up with a joker.

He doesn't know how to respond, so he ignores it. Another beer, and he'll be over the limit.

That evening Marianne, Ana and Rachel head off for a night of dancing at Hodgkinson RSL. When Marianne arrives home at eleven, there's a Christmas present on her doorstep. She knows what it is from the shape – Dior's Hypnotic Poison. Her favourite perfume. She sends Kieran a message.

Thank you for the Chrissie present. I will save it till Christmas Day. Here's a quote for you, as I know you are fond of sayings by Buddha. 'Remember, if you focus on the hurt, you will continue to suffer. If you focus on the lesson, you will continue to grow.'

It is time to stop feeling sorry for yourself and drowning in your own pity. 😊😊 Stand up and fight for the life you want – time to take control. Your friend, Marianne. 😊

On Sunday, Christmas Eve, Kieran catches up with Marianne for breakfast. Their cancelled Christmas plans mean it is too late for her to hook in with her daughter's pre-booked Christmas Day luncheon.

On Christmas morning, Marianne opens her present – alone.

Boxing Day. She hears nothing from Kieran till late at night. It's one of his 'sorry' texts. Apologies won't cut it with her anymore. She feels used. Her index finger jabs the letters on her phone. *I should have spent Christmas with my family just as you are doing. I shouldn't be all by myself. It is so unfair, and all you can say is that you're sorry. I hope everything works out for you and you end up back with your wife if that will make you happy again. Obviously, it isn't me.*

Have you had too much to drink? You have to realise I am scared of ending up on the street. Sorry, I'm so unreliable at the moment.

Rubbish! You are in a far better financial position than I am, and I'm not on the street.

The next day she drives to her daughter's, and the two of them have breakfast at Molly's favourite coffee shop in the Garden City Shopping Centre. Marianne's in dire need of what Ambrosia Café's customer focus dining option has to offer – the decadent, the delicious and the deserved. She's comforted and brightened by the chocolate tones on the walls and the lush, red velvet cushions. She orders freshly baked waffles with butterscotch sauce, caramelised banana and mixed berries. It's another Bridget Jones moment. Usually, she'd go for the savoury option: smashed avocado with poached egg and smoked salmon.

Marianne's son in L.A. sends her flowers with a note: To my number one mother from your number one son. Miss you. x

The next day, Marianne is back home and feeling more positive. It's so glorious to feel wanted, to know how loved she is by her son and daughter, and for them to show it by their actions.

On New Year's Eve, Kieran calls Marianne at eighteen minutes past seven in the morning. By coincidence, their song is playing on the radio – 'Dancing in the Moonlight' by Toploader.

She doesn't answer.

Marianne is looking forward to two nights of parties. Kieran? Well, he's obligingly condemned himself to look after the family dog. No surprises there! He's stuck at home, feeling alone and very isolated. He texts her forty minutes before midnight. There's no reply.

He's desperate for her to call.

He sends a stream of short texts.

Aren't you talking to me? ... Why? ... Please call ... You promised you'd never ghost me.

His phone, expectant, is silent.

His finger is only one centimetre from the call icon, but it might as well be a thousand metres.

Bom Diggy Diggy

Marianne never thought her months would be as they are. December disappears. January tumbles into February, then trembles into March. No 'Happy New Year'; just a relationship stuck in first gear. Make that reverse. How can she and Kieran have come so far, to be further away? The picture of the two of them, the future she saw so clearly, is confused and disjointed. She tries to narrow the distance between them with texts that mix tentative terms of endearment – hun and darlin' – with the everyday.

Sometimes she feels welcome and wanted, at others, discarded and deleted, her love and compassion met with ambivalence and doubt. Kieran's texts no longer include 'darling', not even her name. She's a woman waiting. All she wants is to be with him in that sweet place where they once were. The good times. The dancing times. Not the sad uncertain times.

Marianne hasn't coughed all night, but the only one feeling cheerful and energetic this morning is Marianne's cavoodle, Lulu.

Kieran and Lulu. What a pair! Inseparable mates. He called her his 'Little Shadow'. She hung on his every word.

If Marianne were on the lounge with Kieran, Lulu would put her bottom on Marianne and her head on Kieran. When Marianne was not there, the two of them watched television together. Many evenings he would call Lulu into the kitchen for leftovers. He'd make her sit up. 'Attack-trained killer guard dog number one reporting for duty. Did you chase the cats out of the yard today? No, I didn't think so. How about the big Doberman down the road? Don't tell me, another no. What about the birds in the garden? *What! They chased you.* You are supposed to work for your food. What a disappointment you are. It's just as well you're adorable or you'd starve.'

Marianne knows Kieran's closest mates keep on telling him why he needs to let go of the marriage.

'You're not who you were. Not yourself. You're tense all the time. Disconnected.'

What will it take for him to let go, to move on? She's finding it impossible to continue to hold on to a hope and a prayer. It takes a lot for Marianne to give up. She tells Kieran that he'll end up alone if he leaves the decision too long. He's not having a bar of *that* conversation. He ignores the text. She sends him a photo of herself in a new dress, looking gorgeous in the hallway at home, with the dig that Renata will be happy he is not with her tonight. He ignores the comment, says she looks lovely in the dress and lets her know he is having an evening on his own.

Early March arrives with the sting of a late afternoon horse fly. Marianne feels she's lingered too long in her relationship with Kieran. Maybe it's had its day. Give-up-itis time.

Unexpectedly, Kieran phones her; he wants to come round. "I miss being with you. Holding hands. Kissing, cuddling and talking face to face."

She's over his hit-and-run. "Maybe it's better to wait until you decide where you stand. I love you to death, but I can't deal with this anymore. I can't be a third wheel. I've done everything possible to support you — no hesitation. Yet you continue to shut me out whenever it suits you. If only you could be as tough with Renata as you are with me. She–"

"I–"

"Let me finish. *She* deserves it. *I do not!*"

"I haven't shut you out deliberately. I'm just so sick of talking about Renata."

"I have to go, Kieran." She hangs up.

After a year together, what hits home is that she's still persona non grata. Kieran's nephew, Chris, his sister's son, is getting married in Sydney, an interracial marriage. It's an entire three days of a traditional Indian wedding – Maharani Weddings, Dockside Darling Harbour. She'd love to go, but it's an impossibility. Max will be there, and he still regards her as a homewrecker. Renata won't be there now she and Kieran are separated and close to settlement. Marianne has decided to suitcase her dancing shoes, head up to Langaratta and catch up with her daughter and two crazy grandkids.

When Marianne and Kieran arrive at their respective destinations, she up north and he down south, he sends her a photo of the Lazy Yak Australian pale ale he's drinking. A beer and cheese afternoon with a mate from his high school days. The bottle has a picture of a bull on the label. Shame he can't take the bull by the horns. Marianne googles the beer – 'docile, pleasant and refreshing.' Spot on with the first one. 'Noble beast of burden found in the Himalayas.' Too true, Kieran has more than his fair share of baggage. 'More mild than wild.' Holy Yak! She can see his face on the bottle.

Over the three days of the wedding, Max sets his mum up with a live stream of the videography – a triple feature movie. Renata settles in with a bottle of wine and a cheese platter.

The wedding is a massive affair with one hundred and fifty guests. A Bollywood movie. A marriage on steroids. Vibrant colours, including a handsome man in a fuchsia-pink turban and tie and a soft-pink suit. The ceremony and celebration are indelible flamboyance, energy and exuberance. *Unbelievable* – a fire eater. They do, however, know when to stop. There's no fakir on a bed of nails or a fire walker.

The day before the nuptials, everyone is singing and dancing. There are fireworks. Now, *that's* the absolute joy of an upcoming union. The only song Renata can make out is 'Bom Diggy Diggy'. It sounds as if it's a nursery rhyme about a puppy who digs up flower beds and buries bones.

On the day of the ceremony, the bride arrives looking feminine and beautiful in a red sari with exquisite gold embroidery. Talk about queen for a day. Make that three. Renata cannot imagine any woman *not* looking beautiful as an Indian bride. The bride has half an armful of bangles on each arm and oversize jewellery. She'd make a stunning stand-in for a Christmas tree.

What's not to relish about the intricate henna tattoos on the bride's hands and feet? Besides, Renata knows it's applied at a women's only ceremony. By contrast, she's not so keen on the yellow face painting she saw earlier – presumably turmeric. She's sure it must have some spiritual significance. Still, on an everyday level, its playfulness would surely help alleviate pre-wedding jitters, and act as a reminder of what married life can be like when a toddler comes along.

Renata knows rice is a staple food, but it breaks free from the confines of dinner plates at the ceremony. Puffed rice – Indian popcorn – rises skyward at every opportunity. These people certainly know how to have a good time with family and friends. Maybe that's the secret to being well-behaved at other times: let your hair down in a big way among those you love, and who love you, when it's for a good cause.

There are floral garlands to welcome the bride and groom into each other's families. The wedding ritual includes a prayer to Ganesha. Renata's unsure what a pot-bellied elephant-headed lord has to do with marriage. She checks on Google. He is a harbinger of good fortune, a remover of obstacles.

The ceremony itself is so rich. Additional songs. The bride and groom don't just stand at the altar; they are on an elevated platform surrounded by flowers, metres of opulent silks and pendulous faceted crystals. A fire burns in the centre. Additional puffed rice soars and showers. The bride's brother presents three fistfuls of rice to his sister. The groom places his hands beneath his bride's, sharing the portion with her. As the newly-weds circle the fire *three* times, they offer handfuls of rice to the fire – happiness, prosperity, fertility. More rice is tossed, a lamp lit and garlands worn. Then, the bride and groom are tied together, her veil to his sash. It is not a symbol of servitude but friendship, the basis of a Hindu marriage. A bond made in heaven and supposed to last for seven lifetimes.

As Renata watches the live streaming, it's tough to see Kieran, but at least *that other woman* is not there.

Renata has an 'a-ha' moment when she sees the groom apply a red dot to the centre of his bride's forehead. So that's it! It signifies a woman is married.

Then the reception, a Bollywood extravaganza of song, dance, food, speeches. The reception is a flash mob dance party without the dispersion at the end. First, there's a Bollywood dance by seven women, followed by a dance by eight men. The finale is two dance duets by the bride and groom.

Renata's exhausted from watching it all. Even the three-tier wedding cake has a cutting song. Renata heads to bed before the wedding guests. It's ten p.m.

As she showers, old resentments rise.

There was that one time. A make or break it time about two years ago, before Kieran met his rock 'n' roll-between-the-sheets chick. It involved her husband, another man, a dinner date, an emerald green dress and a bucket of ice. It was the only time Kieran made a stand.

He had joined the dots of a possible infidelity:

her phone always on silent,

staying late at work,

doing an extra salsa class,

spending longer in front of the mirror.

One Thursday night, he turned up at a class, did the class and, at the end of the lesson, warned the guy off. He was very restrained and discrete, the sanctity of marriage and all that.

Was she having an affair?

It was casual flirting. A brief fling.

That weekend Kieran suggested he and she go out for an intimate dinner. Patch things up. She got all dolled up. Her long blonde hair tonged to shiny straightness, Dior 'Rouge Revival' lipstick, and a killer fitted green dress that looked as if she'd been sewn into it. A pair of single pear-drop emerald earrings he had brought her one Christmas. A red clutch bag and stilettoes to match.

It's still raw and vivid for her, how, when she came down the stairs, he looked as if he didn't know what to do with her. He had no words; however, the look he gave her was that of a petrified learner driver at a busy junction looking for a clear safe way forward.

She felt deflated. Stupid. A clown.

All through dinner, they resembled two people starving in a room with an enormous feast. There was no lingering look, no light touch. A fiasco. She knew then that their marriage didn't have a snowball's chance in hell of lasting.

She remembered wanting to drown herself in bubbles, so she asked for a second bottle of Dom Perignon Champagne. No. That's not true. She wanted something more than that. Invalidated, she wanted to demand something she knew he would not want to give. She wanted to start a fight. The 'no' came as did the contents of the ice bucket into his lap. The muscles in her neck rigid, she spat in his ear the words, "*I hate you! You're pathetic!*" before turning, leaving the restaurant and catching a taxi home. That's when their lives truly became fury and silence.

Renata finishes her shower with a thirty-second surge of cold water over her face and body. Her heart rate slows, and the unwanted tension from her thoughts dissipates into calm.

Her sleep is restless and troubled.

Her dreams juxtapose a meagre 'his and her only' registry marriage in black-and-white – her belly swollen – with the extravaganza and dazzling colours of a Hindu ceremony with family and friends.

When Renata wakes in the morning, she is full of spite.

She recalls the story of the man who bought a house next door to his ex-wife and installed a four-metre bronze statue of a hand with its middle finger raised. Oh, the pleasure of destroying someone's waking view.

PART THREE

Stuck in the August Rain

March, fourteen months after Kieran's first date with Marianne, and he moves the last of his belongings out of the marital home. Not without troubled waters, though. Financially sorted is very different from emotionally sorted. Renata won't let go. She continues to call him 'my husband', asks him if he still has feelings for her. Not once does he bad mouth her. Not once does he call her on it.

As April nudges into May, Kieran's settlement comes through, and he moves in with Marianne. They are considering buying a house together and a camper trailer for weekends away. Overseas holidays? Unlike Marianne, Kieran has seen most of the world, but he'd be open to another off the beaten track walking trip to a corner of Italy he hasn't explored; something that's a mixture of nature, culture and coast and at a pace his Mara Mia would enjoy.

Marianne wakes up feeling so blessed to have her beloved man beside her every morning. She goes to bed feeling the same. She drives home from work on a full tank of happy contentment; Kieran will be waiting for her at home. The simple delight of sharing a beer, talking about their day and then, cooking dinner together. A perfect life. Here at last. Worth all the ups and downs. *Hallelujah*!

Marianne is on a cruise for four days in June, Saturday to Tuesday, with her daughter, the two grandkids, and her son-in-law, Callum. The four-year-old, Oliver, is as reliable as a digital alarm clock. He attempts to wake her as soon as the sky curtains light grey. Trying to hang on to precious moments of sleep, she pretends she hasn't noticed. Like a puppy, he places his face right next to hers. She can smell his light sweet breath mingled with impatience. The smile on her lips does not reach her eyes.

"Jamjar, I need a hug."

It's what he's called her since he could pronounce his j's but not his gr's. She has never questioned it, coming from a child who, for some unfathomable reason, called his mother's breasts 'ninnies'. Oliver prises Marianne's left eye open. Reluctantly, she opens the other and puts her arm out. He nestles in. Thank goodness. She can close her eyes again. However, there's no respite for her ears; an unstoppable stream of chatter assaults her usual morning bliss.

"I'm hungry ... Can I watch TV? ... I've got Superman PJs ... Get up, Jamjar."

At least he doesn't have a bear as does his six-year-old sister, Ally. A bear that sings intermittently throughout the sleeping hours. Marianne has that pleasure tomorrow night.

She *just* wants five more minutes. "See the clock, Oli. When the long hand is on the one, I will get up."

As he looks past her to the clock on the bedside table, he lies on his stomach, his head in the vee of his hands. It seems to be taking a long time. He turns his gaze to her face. "How old are you?"

"I'm not sure, Oli."

"Look in your undies, Jamjar. I am four to six."

She hopes he won't offer to check out her undies. She'd have a hard time explaining why she's ten. He'd give her that look that means he knows something isn't quite right. He'd pause ... then another question. She can hear it now.

"Did you start at zero?"

And, so it always goes with him – funny little tacker.

Ally. She's a sweet child, the spitting image of Marianne at that age – all smiles and blonde curls. Such patience and determination. For some time, she'd refused to learn to tie her shoelaces. It drove Molly nuts. "You're going to fall over one day all because of your laces." When that didn't work, she told Ally that the escalator's teeth would eat her up if her laces ever caught.

Molly never did get to tell her daughter, 'I told you so!'

One day – *shazam*! Ally was gluing brightly coloured feathers on a papier-mâché bird for a school project, her tongue poking out in concentration.

"Do you need help?" Marianne had asked.

"No, Grandma. I can do it."

As Marianne laughed and looked down, she noticed that one of Ally's shoelaces was undone.

"What about your shoelace?"

Ally grabbed the plastic tip at the end of each lace and stuck it into the eyelet below, where the lace threaded through on either side. It held the loops in place so her fingers didn't need to. She wrapped one loop over the other and pulled the laces together. As she pulled the laces tight, she wrapped one of the loops in the other a second time – a sturdy double knot.

"Who taught you that?"

"Me."

OMG. Genius. Bunny ears, cheerio!

When Marianne and Oli head to the continental buffet breakfast they are the first to arrive. No surprises there. Oli chooses the mixed fresh fruit with yoghurt. It's so sweet to see the tip of his nose with a dollop of yoghurt as he asks her what they are going to do today. Wipe your cute little nose for a start, buddy.

Meanwhile, Kieran is at a Byron Bay farmstay for a blokey weekend singing around the campfire, bushwalking and fishing with some of his mates. The morning sky has an amber glow tinged yellow at the edges as it radiates from the horizon like a distant wildfire.

Life is better uncomplicated. He appreciates that Marianne always supports him doing things separately or together. She gets him – unity, autonomy.

And so, their shared life passes till, one midday blue and cloudless Tuesday in early July, they both file for divorce. There are no real hiccups except that Kieran makes a mistake with the divorce application and must lodge an affidavit. The whole process is doing his head in. The mistake? The place of marriage. Boy, would Renata have a field day with that if she knew? 'You always ... you never ...' She's a dab hand at weaponising past mistakes.

The next day, both divorces are finalised. In celebration, Marianne gives Kieran a book of sayings: *You Are My Once In A Lifetime*. He takes her out shopping for a diamond cluster ring. It's modest, but she's never owned one.

"Oh, Kieran. *It's beautiful.*"

At that moment, each is a tidal flow of life and love.

Smooth waters from now on.

When Marianne wakes the following day, she's fatigued. A disturbed night with Kieran up and down like a jack-in-the-box.

"You're getting up a lot in the night? Can't you sleep?"

"It's not that. I just need to go even though not much comes."

"Wee, you mean?"

"Yea. Same in the day."

She discovers it has been going on since May. "Hun, you need to get it checked out." She knows that in men a urinary tract infection is already a reason to be referred to a urologist. Marianne has to be on his case for over two months to get him to see his doctor. *Men.* Why do they prefer to ignore things? Always hanging on to the hope that time makes medical problems disappear.

After continuous antibiotics for three months, there's no improvement. No way is it an infection. It pains him to pee, and again, his back is a bothersome burden. He hides an itchy feeling in his stomach, scratching it furtively when she's not around or anyone else for that matter.

Marianne pulls strings and gets him an immediate between-patients appointment with his doctor. She provides Kieran with the name of the top urologist he needs a referral for – Doctor Aadarsh Dawar, Harbourville. Marianne's now doing what she does best – 'Little Miss Organiser'. Thank goodness she knows how the system works; otherwise, it would be next year before an appointment with a urologist is available.

As soon as Kieran confirms the referral, Marianne organises an appointment. With a little bit of charm, professional pressure and an obliging receptionist, she's given an appointment for the next day. Thursday midday.

Kieran is not doing so well: several cancelled destressing paddling sessions due to lack of numbers, plus he's only recently sorted out marital matters, and *now* he has to deal with something else.

"Best pack an overnight bag, hun. Sometimes a surgeon might want to operate straight away."

"Should I be worried?"

"No, just prepared. When we go for a trip up north, you always say pack plenty of water, a snack and a pee pot, as you never know if there'll be a traffic holdup due to an accident on the highway."

The thing about being a medical receptionist, she can't pull the wool over her own eyes, but for now she can pull it over his. She has a terrible sense of foreboding of what lies on the other side of this.

That night in bed, they are both unsettled.

Over breakfast Marianne fishes. "You were calling out in the night, Kieran. Bad dreams?"

"What did I say?"

"You were talking to someone. You said 'no' a few times."

"I can't remember the details. I do remember I was in my mother's house. She was showing me the rooms. She died when I was in my thirties. No idea why she was in my dream as a tour guide."

Marianne doesn't share what has unsettled her. Best not to. She thought she saw two shadowy figures of an elderly couple standing by Kieran's side of the bed. Was stress making her see things? She'd opened and closed her eyes repeatedly. Although they disappeared, a dark, dense dread lodged in her solar plexus like indigestion.

It's an early start on the Thursday. At such short notice, they have nowhere to leave Lulu; she'll be at home on her own – not ideal. She's a nervy little thing, but there's no choice. In case they are away overnight, Marianne leaves a full food and water bowl.

They make the trip in an hour and a half.

Doctor Dawar is running to schedule.

He is a stocky middle-aged man with rimless glasses, kind chocolatey eyes and a soft voice. Marianne takes it as a good sign that the fern in his room is flourishing.

He listens attentively to Kieran and Marianne before he responds.

"I need to do a cystoscopy. It's an exploratory procedure. Nothing to cause concern. A tube with a tiny video camera is threaded into your urethra and bladder so I can view your bladder lining and take a biopsy. It will give me a clear indication of what's going on."

"How soon can you do it? When is your next list?"

"I'm operating tomorrow, Marianne."

"Any room in there for Kieran?"

"Yes."

"Brilliant. Thank you so much. May I have five minutes with Kieran in private?"

Doctor Dawar leaves the room.

Marianne takes charge, as Kieran's hesitancy is palpable. "Kieran, you're better off getting it done. If there is something wrong, early intervention is vital. Are you prepared to pay as a private patient for this? It will be about three-and-a-half thousand."

"That's a lot of money!"

"Kieran, you need to consider what your life is worth. If I tell him you're self-funded, you'll be in tomorrow. As a public patient, you may have a six-month wait at the very least. You're far from being short of money. Let's get it done. Yes?"

He nods just as Dawar enters.

"Did I give you two enough time?"

"Perfect timing. We'll go ahead and pay for the surgery so there's no delay."

"My receptionist will give you a print-out of the costs. Kieran will need to stay overnight so we can do blood tests, an MRI and the paperwork for the hospital admission."

Kieran's on the list for the procedure early Friday afternoon.

Marianne leaves before dawn on Friday when the sky is charcoal and the air chilled with a silent steady breath. She flicks on the radio, but there is no ease for her in either silence or song. Tears cataract her pupils and collect on the rim of her lower eyelids. Her saliva thickens. Get a grip, girl. She wants to scream, to pummel the steering wheel with her fists. She pulls over. Her tears flood in rage and grief. She needs someone to hold her. She's drowning in emotion. Her body is hot and cold simultaneously. Blood pounds in her temples.

When her self-control returns, Marianne starts the car and pulls back onto the highway. With her windows rolled down, she concentrates on the road, the day outside and relaxes as best she can into the rush of air on her face and hair.

On the hands-free, she leaves a voice message to cancel her and Kieran's attendance at the 'Rewind Rock 'N' Roll Weekend' that starts tomorrow. Immediately, there's an incoming call.

"Hi, Marianne. Are you cancelling because of what happened yesterday with my son?"

"I don't know what you mean, Lorraine. I've been in Harbourville."

"Oh! My son lives diagonally across the road from you. He's a shift worker. Your dog wouldn't stop barking, so he went over and banged on your door. He started yelling and swearing. Lost his temper when you didn't answer and dented your fence with his foot."

What the hell? Just what Marianne doesn't need – minor shit. "Look, Lorraine. I'm dealing with an emergency at the moment. I'm on my way home now. I'll sort it out later."

When Marianne arrives home and opens the door to her villa, Lulu is a total mess. Faeces all over her and on the floor at the front door. As Marianne cleans up, her tears are a dripping tap, her movements leaden. When she makes herself a cup of tea, she notices that a fly, which buzzed against the kitchen window the day they left, is feet up on the window ledge. She sucks it up into the tomb of the dustbuster.

It's almost four in the afternoon when Marianne arrives back at the hospital; the time of day when the sun sinks pale and weary on the horizon. The 'will-thrive-anywhere' monstera in the hospital foyer is struggling to survive, its edges browned and crisp.

Although in a public hospital, Marianne finds Kieran in a private room away from the other patients. Dawar needs to talk to them both. He hands Marianne a box of tissues. Kieran wonders how he knows that airless rooms make her sneeze.

Kieran hopes for everything, expects the results to reveal nothing. Marianne waits for the two words that take a mere two seconds to say; two simple words with the power to destroy a long-imagined future. Both are still and silent.

Doctor Dawar's words etch into the day. "I'm sorry ..."

Kieran can't hear past the apology. He sees Dawar's mouth moving, but it's a silent movie. The heartburn of a breath catches in Kieran's chest. The room becomes airless, and it's as if the padded armchair he's sitting in increases in size as he shrinks and is swallowed by it.

The rest of Dawar's words come with the ease and compassion of the frequently rehearsed. How many patients has he given a cancer diagnosis to? The odd one in a hundred? Hundreds? A thousand?

"... Kieran. You have an extremely rare and aggressive form of bladder cancer that is muscle-invasive. It is embedded in the lining of your bladder. Do you understand what I'm saying?"

Kieran sits. Shocked. Silent. Trawling for questions might uncover truths that he does not want to hear. His stomach is an empty steel drum – hollow.

For Marianne, the diagnosis is more confirmation than revelation. She had sensed cancer would come calling, as one day when Kieran was in bed on his back sleeping, she'd glanced over at him only for the details of his face to become those of her dad's as he battled with cancer. At that moment, she knew her dad was preparing her for what was to come.

"I have done a Transurethral Resection of the Bladder and removed the tumour. That will give me the tumour type, stage and grading so we know what we're dealing with. You'll need further tests to see if it has spread elsewhere outside the wall."

Dawar looks at Kieran. Though spoken evenly and softly, he's aware his words are a rusty scalpel that slices and tears.

Elsewhere. The word hovers above Marianne as a phantom echo. She and Kieran have only been living together for a measly three months. The room suddenly feels cold. She shivers. *Please, please, don't let it be in the surrounding tissue.* What Kieran has, holds the potential of a terminal number – stage four cancer. She's catastrophising again. It's what she does when she's overwhelmed.

Rage, a thermal king tide, rises in Marianne. She's aware of spiritual laws: the spill of chronic unresolved emotional trauma into the physical – a perfect carcinogenic storm. Fifty percent of bladder cancers are caused by smoking. Kieran's *never* been a smoker; however, his life *has been* a smouldering cigarette for years.

Kieran makes a silent pledge with the news: remain in hope despite the odds. After all, treatments are continually improving. One step at a time.

"We'll need to follow up in a few weeks to check your progress. You'll also need to start a series of chemotherapy sessions once a week to target any rogue cells. I will ring your local hospital to let them know so they're able to arrange a schedule as soon as possible."

Kieran turns to Marianne. "Marianne, I need you to ring Max. I can't do it. I'll break down."

"Of course, I will, hun," is what she says, but she wonders how Max will respond, as it will be the first time she's spoken to him. "Hi, Max. It's Marianne, your dad's partner. Your dad has asked me to ring you. He's had surgery, but it's not good news."

"May I to speak to my father?"

"I am not trying to prevent that, Max, but right now your dad is in shock. He's a mess. It's rare for him to break down and show his emotions in such a raw physical way. Give him a day or two back in Cavendish Bay – she's careful not to say 'back home'– and I know he will want to speak to you himself. He asked me to ring because he wanted you to be the first to know."

She knows Kieran doesn't want to talk about the diagnosis. Why did he have to be the one in one hundred-and-eight men who get it before the age of seventy-five? Why did it have to be the type that's only one percent of all cases? So, so unfair for a man as healthy and fit as Kieran. She will have to dig deep. Find the strength to support him. She wishes she could swallow the doctor's words so the steel and stone of them would sink to a depth where the ears no longer hear.

Around eleven a.m. the next day, after a cuppa and a sandwich, Kieran is sent home, the catheter still in place. He's not long home when he starts complaining of a sore calf. Marianne wonders if he has a blood clot, but the specialist is insistent it's not possible. Kieran is lucky. He has an appointment with Doctor Brysk, the oncologist, at a quarter-to-three. Brysk by name and brisk by nature, she rarely smiles, but what she lacks in bedside manner she makes up for in reputation. That's the bottom line for Marianne. Besides, Tom Devere the radiotherapy oncologist they've been allocated has smiles enough for two. Doctor Brysk writes Kieran a referral for a PET scan and a Doppler. She marks it 'high priority' and rings Shoreline Radiology to ensure Kieran is first up the next day. She prescribes a regime of Clexane injections once a day to prevent blood clots. Marianne's impressed; Kieran is in good hands.

The results are through before morning tea. Not only is there a clot in Kieran's calf, but there's also a huge one in his groin.

That night he's in excruciating pain. Marianne takes him and his catheter to the local hospital. There are a series of serious complications – clots in his leg, clots in his bladder, and bleeding. The hospital ups the dosage of the blood thinner Doctor Brysk prescribed and discharges him.

Kieran struggles for the entire first three weeks in July. Marianne has done all she can to get him the best medical help as quickly as possible. All the medical information she has to absorb is a bombardment that overwhelms her with responsibility and self-doubt. Is she up to this?

Marianne desperately needs support herself. She continues to struggle with all the pre-divorce drama Renata created in Marianne's relationship with Kieran – mind-games, misinformation and lies. However, there's another layer to the rejection and abandonment Marianne has to navigate. It's a twenty-eight-year-old layer: the cancer stuff she went through with her dad. From diagnosis to death, he lasted seven months. Her daughter was five. Marianne conceived Liam the day of her dad's diagnosis. That was *always* her first husband's fix for any problem – sex. In hindsight, she is stunned that her marriage lasted twenty years.

She carries, always, the guilt of not doing more for her much-loved dad. A man who made her feel loved, secure and cherished. She adored him. The timing was all wrong. He was too young, and she had the demands of work, pregnancy and a young child.

On a day in late July, approaching four-thirty in the afternoon, Marianne is emptying the dishwasher. The last rays of the western sun over the rooftop reflect through the kitchen window onto the stainless-steel lid of the kettle as a blinding star-burst of piercing light. With the evening coo of a distant bird and the dying light, what's hiding becomes intolerably clear to her. As clear as the fact that she has been to the hospital's emergency department twice today. Life has got it all wrong. It's cheated her. Enjoying the simple things with him by her side – conversation, walks, movies, dancing – was not meant to play out this way. His toothbrush was supposed to lie side by side with hers. The gentle teasing over which way the toilet roll should unravel, the playful tussle over the remote and persuasions over which channel to watch on the television were meant to continue.

She knows she has to unhook herself from these thoughts. If she doesn't, she'll drown in an imagined future.

The next day, Friday, is crisp and sunny. A community nurse comes to the villa to remove Kieran's catheter and do a bladder scan. While she is doing this, Marianne inspects the Colourbond fence and checks the mailbox. Boy, it's a wonder he didn't break his foot. There's a note in her letterbox, an apology. She opens it, reads, and as she folds it and looks up, Lorraine's son is heading towards her from across the road.

"I can't apologise enough. My anger got the better of me. Sleep deprivation as a shift worker and reason goes out the window. I'll see to getting it fixed."

It's of little importance to Marianne. A pristine home is no longer a priority.

On the last Sunday in July, Kieran is in pain again. She drives him to his doctor. A urinary tract infection from the catheter. More antibiotics. That night he's admitted to the hospital yet again – pain urinating. He's discharged the next day.

Kieran's early hours, days, and nights become 'revolving door syndrome' – *at* home, *in* hospital.

On a Monday four days before July merges into August, Kieran sees Tom Devere, the radiotherapy oncologist. Two days later, Kieran is taken to hospital by ambulance at five-thirty in the morning. Trouble from the previous day: blockages, and bleeding from the sides of his penis where the catheter was inserted on Sunday. Nothing seems to be working, him or the treatments. On Friday, there's a second surgery to try to stem the bleeding. Kieran nicknames the hospital 'The Vampire's Den'. There's no hospital discharge, as he remains far from stable.

The next three days are his first chemo session, minor blockages in the night that pass clots, more antibiotics and nausea. He's amazed that the anti-nausea medication is a dead ringer for a communion wafer. A wafer left to melt on the tongue feels like a treat amongst a pharmacological diet of pills and infusions.

Then comes the in and out of 'Hokey Cokey' days. Except it's not about turning things all around, and it doesn't involve smiles and good times on the dance floor.

Out: Thirteen days after surgery, Kieran is discharged.

In: Within six days, the clots start. He's back waiting in emergency for four hours. Five p.m. is a lousy timeslot – the walking wounded.

Out: He's sent home with the familiar regime of Clexane injections. His stomach has become a daily pin cushion. He's never carried much fat, so Marianne fights to find enough excess to pinch into a ridge to inject. He has a nickname for this too – 'Needle Ping Pong'. The injection site alternates daily on either side of his belly button.

In: Four days later, Monday, he is back in the hospital. Bleeding and deep vein thromboses. Will this never let up? It's insane, the unrelenting ooze and congeal. *Give the man a break!*

Out: Discharged after a day's surgical watch. He looks drawn and ashen.

In: A week later, on Wednesday at eight-thirty in the morning, he's back in the emergency department with deep vein thromboses and bleeding.

Kieran says jokingly about it all, "Maybe I should leave my coffee cup here permanently."

His half-joke, half-serious quip makes Marianne's heart bleed. It's always his strategy when he's nervous, or in this case, terrified – act normal, act light.

She smiles. "Seems that way, babe."

Kieran is now a prisoner of this disease. Parole. Report tri-weekly. By the way, here are twelve rounds of chemotherapy three days a week, for four weeks.

By mid-August, days are relentless in their pace: appointments, scans, test results, follow-ups. Marianne is now his personal assistant.

Most days are much the same as her diary entry for one day:

8:30 – Centrelink (Carers Allowance. Aged Pension)

12:00 – Accountant

1:30 – Hospice, Communication Engagement Officer

3:30 – Psychologist (me)

4:30 – GP (Kieran)

And so it goes. On ... and ... on. Over ... and ... over.

She won't leave him alone in the villa, as she fears something might happen to him when she's not there. If anything did, the burden of guilt would be too much for her to bear. Also, she doesn't want him to feel lonely. The solution is to cut her work back to three days a week – Thursday, Friday, Saturday – three-to-four hours a day max.

As things progress, she knows she will have to use all her leave: holiday, sick and long service. She is fierce in securing Kieran the best possible chance of fighting this. She feels the pressure of the responsibility for making the right decisions. At times she rages against his ex-wife for always threatening to walk away, but not wanting Kieran to because it meant she had lost control over him. Marianne's sure she never knew the half of it. Gentlemen don't blab. *What a heartless fucking bitch!* Years of abuse – emotional and sometimes physical. Suffocation. Shame. Anxiety. Fear. Depression. Loss of self-worth. All of this had grown and metastasised with the same level of severe toxicity as their source. Dark spaces imprisoned in the spirit become dark splotches on scans.

She can't be angry with a sick man for his indecision.

Self-contained, Kieran shares none of what he is going through with anyone. Determined cancer will not bring him down, he drags himself out of the door to work. Desperate for old routines, he avoids stillness at all costs, as it allows space for the void of dread and despair.

On the Monday of the week following his discharge, Marianne gets a call from Kieran's boss.

"Hello, Marianne. It's Melvin, Kieran's boss. I hope you don't object to my ringing you. Kieran has you down as his close contact."

"That's fine. Is everything okay?"

"Yes. I am sure you know Kieran told us yesterday he was ill, working his way through it but wants to stay at work. I just want you to know we will support him to the hilt. He's a highly valued member of our small company. He's been with us for twenty years. You can always rely on him for meeting deadlines, his eye for detail and his dry sense of humour. As long as he wants to come in, we're behind him one hundred percent. There'll be no pressure. He can do what he can. If he spends parts of the day dozing, we already have that covered. We've replaced his chair with one of the most comfortable gaming chairs we could find. He chuckled when we told him the name of it – Noblechairs 'Hero' Series.

Marianne manages to hold her composure long enough to thank him for his care of Kieran and consideration for her. How many companies would do that for an employee? That someone other than herself is actively looking out for him, brings her to tears.

It's now the sixth day since the hospital discharged Kieran.

The deep vein thromboses are back.

Another admission. Surgical watch for a day and a night. Another discharge.

He's dredged of energy and just wants to sleep, but there are more tests, and Max is due to visit for three days.

Before Kieran's discharge, Doctor Dawar comes to see him. He's rung Marianne to tell her to be there, as he needs to speak to them both to be sure Kieran understands what he has to say. Marianne pushes for more. Dawar refuses to engage.

When Dawar enters Kieran's room, they see from his knotted lips and smile of strained sympathy that the diagnosis is terrible. There is no shrink and disappear – he's a medico, not a magician.

Kieran begins to tremble, and his breathing is that of a helpless hooked creature flaying on the shoreline. He is unprepared for what's coming.

"It's not good news. The cancer has grown back. It's twice as big." He says it softly, but it hits with the force of a bullet at close distance.

Marianne's mouth is dry as if she's lost the ability to breathe through her nose.

Dizzy, she faints.

She wakes up in a hospital bed in a foetal position within the folds of three warm waffle blankets. Oh, how she wants to stay there forever, cocooned away from this world of woe. Kieran is sitting limply in the chair next to the bed.

Back home, Marianne prepares for Max's visit tomorrow. Renata will pick him up from the airport. He plans to catch up with his father for breakfast and a beach walk. However, when Max sees Kieran's deterioration, he understands why Marianne has prepared breakfast for them. There will be no walk on the beach.

Marianne leaves the two of them together and nips out to do some supermarket shopping. When she comes back, Kieran is dozing, and Max is on his phone.

Before Max leaves, Marianne slips him a letter. "Please read it when you get home and when you are in a good spot emotionally."

Max doesn't wait till he gets home. He drives his mother's car to the beach and sits with his back against a warm rock.

Hi, Max.

Firstly, I wanted to take this time to say how very sorry I am that your dad has cancer. My dad also had cancer, so I do have some idea of all the mixed emotions and fears you are going through at the moment. I want you to know that I care deeply for your dad. I will be there no matter what the outcome. I will do everything in my power to look after him to ensure his journey is as smooth as possible. I hope we can all work together for your dad's sake.

I know it is not easy for you to accept our relationship. You believe that I am the reason your parents did not stay together. Your dad is a strong, loyal and loving man. He has never said a bad word about your mother to me and has never shared his side of the story with you for fear of losing you more than he already feels he has.

I fell in love with a miserable man. A broken man filled with remorse and guilt that his marriage had failed. Only the caring and conscientious feel this. They are just two of the qualities your dad has.

I would never have gotten involved in a marriage break-up. I would not want it done to me, so I would never do that to another woman.

When your dad and I started seeing each other, he and your mum had lived separate lives in the same house for two years. The marriage was beyond fixing.

I know the depth of the love your dad has for you, so whether your mum and dad are together or apart, it will make no difference to the love they each share for you.

I am not here to take anything away from your mum. I am not a gold digger. I own my own modest home and am financially independent.

Your dad and I love one another, and I just simply want to share my life with him. I don't expect you to like me, but I would like to believe that we can be respectful to one another so your dad does not have to deal with the added stress of warring parties who can't communicate. We all need to pull together.

Despite our differences, we have one thing in common: the knowledge that Kieran is the most important person to support and protect at this moment in time. His journey will be that of an everyday hero. You know him. He will never complain and will cling to hope, for this is the only way he can reconcile himself to this awful diagnosis.

So please, Max, let us focus on what is important and work together.

Regards,

Marianne.

As Max finishes the letter, a fine crack appears on the porcelain of the truth his mother has told him. The light of another reality begins to shine through. Marianne is *not* the wicked whore of the west.

Give and Take

How do you dismantle a man? Part by part. Month by month. Remove what no longer works on the inside and make the inside's private mechanics visible on the outside. Check how that has all tried to save him and then ... then ... when attempts to save the dismantled man have failed, try, try, again. This is how it is for Kieran.

Dr Brysk and the oncology care team discuss a clinical trial.

September, October and November have no mornings. They have mournings. Mournings of the lost, the unwelcome, the unwanted. Desperate days.

Routines remain, just not the routines of old.

As well as a coffee before work, Marianne gives Kieran his Clexane injection. When she's at work, her new schedule is to check by text how he's doing at various points throughout the day: arrival, morning tea break, lunch, afternoon tea break, before she leaves. Her messages include reminders for his medication and medical appointments, but also affirmations to let him know that she loves him.

I love you in the morning, in the middle of the day, in the hours we're together and the hours we are apart. – Anon. Please remember that, hun.

Sometimes her texts are simply reminders of domestic trivia.

Hi, hun. I'll pick up schnitzel from the butcher around the corner from work.

Now, when Kieran brushes his teeth at night, he does so by the light from the hallway, with the door pulled shut just enough for Lulu to sneak through. He does this because he does not want to see what he has become. A reflection can be a cruel thing. He has lost his hair, and his skin has a grey tone. The bones beneath his dull eyes give them a sunken look. The flesh beneath his upper arms is slack.

On good days, he meets mates for lunch; he can get himself together by that time of the day. Sometimes friends come to the villa and sit on the newly-built deck to chat about times past.

Mentioning decks, persuading Kieran to contribute half to the cost of building the modest deck – spacious enough for a table of six and a Weber Baby Q barbeque – had been on par with 'The Throwaway' issue on the dance floor. Marianne considered her request fair, as with the two of them there the living room was at capacity with one visitor. She knew he'd want his mates round sometimes, and then there was his sister, Claire, and her husband, Morris and of course, Max.

Today's a perfect example of the benefits of having the deck. Col, an old mate who played in a band with Kieran when they were in their early twenties, is out there sharing a beer with Kieran in the fresh air and sunshine.

Kieran was the strummer and Col the singer.

"Remember the roadie rule – if it moves, root it. If it doesn't, put it in the truck."

"Yes, in those days, Col, you did have relationship wanderlust."

"Trust you to make it sound so bloody polite. I was forever being asked, 'Are you having sex with anyone else?' I'd say no and make sure I never saw the one who asked again."

"You know me, a one-woman man. Now you, as lead singer, with Jim Morrison looks, well, the roadies didn't get a look-in."

"One-woman man? How about nil. We all know, no one sleeps with the banjo player. Mind you. I'm no Lothario now. Why is it when we get older, we get uglier? Now, when I try to come on to women, they give me the look of a toddler being told to eat a brussel sprout."

Col is shocked by how Kieran looks, but he knows better than to mention it. As great a mate as Kieran is, he's very private about some things. Best to wait till he's ready to share. Besides, sometimes when you're seriously ill, all you want is to feel the bond of friendship and chat about things that you can wrap your laughing gear around.

That night Kieran has a bad dream. It's someone other than Col saying the roadie rule. Someone who feels as if they are a friend. Kieran listens, he hears the word 'trunk'. He looks into the friend's eyes, into the blackness of them. He knows this friend has come to kill him. When their eyes collide again, each knows the other knows this. The friend says, "You know. Don't you?" The dream does not rouse Kieran from his sleep, but his breathing becomes shallow and rapid as his body registers dream paralysis. There is no point in trying to run. Surrender is all there is.

When he awakes in the morning, he has no memory of the dream; nevertheless, it lingers unsettled in his body.

Before the final fourth round of chemo begins, Claire and Morris visit for a few days. All Kieran wants to do is lie down and rest. That's how most of his days are now. It's by the sheer force of his will that he continues to work.

There's another emergency admission at one in the morning, eight days later. Kieran celebrates his September birthday in hospital not with lit candles but with blood loss. Despite this, he's pleased Marianne's daughter and the grandkids have come down from Boondock to spend the day with her. His wonderful, loving woman needs a break. She sends him the best birthday present she can.

Happy birthday to my one and only incredible man. I love you. xxxx

Despite what is going on, those last five words are the icing on his non-existent cake.

October turns the sweet to sour. Doctor Dawar has no choice but to remove Kieran's bladder and create a urinary diversion via a urostomy pouch. The surgery is radical. Forty-five lymph nodes are removed from Kieran's groin. Four are cancerous, margins clear.

Nine days after surgery, Kieran is discharged.

The stoma nurse is composed and sympathetic. She takes Marianne aside, "We are a backstop. Call any hour."

Marianne wonders how many little deaths her precious man can die before he is defeated and crushed.

But there is more. *Always more.*

Within four days, as October edges towards November, the bleeding begins anew, and the tumescence in his penis would be worthy of a porn star if it did not make him feel like 'The Elephant Man'. It's the same with his feet.

Oedema.

That he takes all this without complaint is a tragedy and a tribute. Although he is weak, he resists help. To receive bad news is now beyond shock and collapse; it's become the expected.

His body no longer smells like his. He starts jokingly calling himself Stinking Stanley when there are accidents with the pouch. The first time he calls himself this, Marianne's heart space fills with tender compassion, and, on the verge of tears, she turns to him and looks him in the eyes. "Don't say that, hun. You will always be the same sweet man to me." Her sunlit tenderness is infinite – sky, air and ocean.

She knows his half-jests, half-serious nicknames are his attempts to circumnavigate a mind constantly trying to drag him into a future that terrifies him.

By silent and progressive stealth, cancer has its way. Its guerrilla tactics win out over modern medicine. Kieran is coughing up blood, and sometimes his breath catches in his chest, rendering him wordless.

He has a CT scan of his chest.

There are secondaries in his lungs.

Another appointment with Doctor Dawar.

Marianne looks at the devouring glowing spots on the imaging of the latest CT scan that Doctor Dawar is showing her. It's unbearably clinically evident to Marianne that Kieran's cancer, without a medical miracle, is heading towards a death sentence.

Dawar knows Marianne is pressing him for a 'tell it like it is', but it's transparent to him that his patient prefers not to know. Some people can't handle brutal truths; knowing them robs them of the time they could have. He's been a first-hand witness to that. It seems hard and inhumane to face someone with a truth they do not want to hear. It's also lethal. They crumble and collapse. Patients who should have eighteen months, gone in two. Hope is purpose. Loss of hope is death. Of course, others embrace an end date with relief and gratitude because they want to know the 'when' and 'how'. 'How?' is the big one. We all want a painless death. This man slumped before him is not ready for either the 'when' or the 'how'. He wants the 'what next'.

On the third of December, Doctor Brysk tells Kieran that he's been approved to partake in a clinical trial – Pembrolizumab. An immunotherapy treatment every fortnight to enhance the natural cancer-fighting capabilities of his immune system. Ultimately, Marianne knows they are just buying time.

During that week, Kieran clears out his desk, filing cabinet and bookshelf at work. Some of the things are forty years old. He will bring everything home in boxes. He's not ready for a no-return policy that discarding and shredding will acknowledge. He continues to work despite Marianne's earnest, ultimately yielding, opposition.

After work at the Wharf Hotel, he meets the boys from soccer, followed by an Indian dinner at Buddha's Belly. There's a text from Marianne as he's about to leave work.

Hi, hun. I am held up at the dog groomers. They are running late. Can't pop in to work and say hello before you leave for the pub. Love you heaps. xoxo

Maybe I should have dropped Lulu off. I could have had my curls trimmed if they had a two-for-one offer going. Your loving man. 🐕

He's referring to his lost chemo hair which has grown back wavy. One of the other cancer patients told him this would happen, usually temporary. It's got nothing to do with eating your crusts. Astounding, what he was sometimes told as a child. He puts his heightened anxiety as an adult down to his family who told those white lies as did many of the caregivers of his generation. His mum said that if he burped and passed wind simultaneously, he would turn inside out. His dad was no better. He told Kieran that the oil stains on the street were little kids who'd been run over because they didn't hold an adult's hand while crossing the road. Grandma? If you wander off, the boogie man will kill you and make you into sausages. It was a family pattern Kieran did *not* repeat with his son.

In the second week of December, Kieran, Claire and Morris visit Breckonridge for a week; it's a small coastal town with wild beaches and pristine lakes. It's precious family time, but it also provides respite for Marianne. She's coping, but she's put on weight, and her smile does not light up her eyes anymore. The stress she is under is apparent to those who know her, but the extent of the daily trauma hides from them by default because Marianne is too consumed with the doing to explain.

The immunotherapy is scheduled through till May the following year. During this period, Marianne and Kieran both work on and off.

On a Monday, the day before Christmas, Kieran has an appointment with Doctor Brysk.

On the CT images, there are dark spots. Shadows. They should not be there.

The immunotherapy is not working.

Kieran has more metastases in his lungs.

"Can more be done?" is all Kieran asks.

"We can try radiation." Doctor Brysk turns back to her computer screen and scrolls. "The first session would be Sunday, the thirtieth. The two others on the second and third of January next year."

Marianne sits there. All she says is, "That's great news. No treatment over Christmas and New Year's Eve."

It *is* good news, as they have booked into a caravan park twenty minutes north of Cavendish Bay. All the family together. Liam is flying in from Los Angeles. Molly, Callum and the grandkids will be in a camper trailer, and she, Kieran and Liam, in a unit.

Max plans to spend Christmas at his mother's, a five-minute drive away from the caravan park. He'll pop in on Boxing Day. Then, for Marianne and Kieran, Xmas Eve at the local RSL surrounded by music and their dancing buddies. She's emailed a request for the band to play a song from Kieran's favourite band Human Nature – 'Reach Out I'll be There'.

Marianne knows that the preciousness of 'now' will be held in the togetherness of quality time and physical touch.

Time in a Bottle

The beginning of a new year, and Kieran is still a fugitive from the law of averages: he continues to work. He goes through the motions each day of getting up and going to work – groundhog days. Marianne takes care of everything that orbits around his new normal.

Kieran is having a good day today. It's a Friday. The day after Valentine's Day. There's been a euphoric shift. No pain. A hint of his old energy. The freedom that, on this particular day, he is no longer held captive by a bed.

Today, he has two appointments: a Doppler to check for blocked arteries; bloods to check his red and white blood cell counts, his platelets, how well his kidneys and liver are working and whether cancer has spread to the bone. Only now, at sixty-seven, has he discovered that a person who is specialised to take blood is known as a phlebotomist. You learn something new every day.

At 8:30 a.m. he texts Marianne at work. *Can I please have a date with you tonight at DJ Donny's?* He's desperate for anything that is an extension of his former self. Anything that doesn't make him feel a repugnant cast-off.

Sure can. My pleasure, treasure. 🐨

In the evening, Kieran and Marianne go rock 'n' roll dancing at Hodgkinson RSL. The usual crowd is there. Everyone tries to hide their shock behind the usual chit-chat. Kieran's cancer and treatment have aged him ten years; his face is like a well-worn crumpled T-shirt. His hair, beginning to grow back, is alfalfa sprouting's, his blue-grey eyes unlit, and the whites, tinged yellow, have no sparkle. Marianne has put on more weight and is almost chubby. Not enough dancing. Too much stress. So be it. Taking care of Kieran *and* herself – you've got to be joking!

Two years ago, Kieran and Marianne would have whirled the night away, but tonight, after two dances, he sits to ease the tightness and pain in his chest that challenges his ability to breathe. Even sitting down, his breath is a slow struggle to grasp eddies of relief.

While most of the others are on the dance floor, only Rachel dares sit down on the empty chair next to him and ask him how he's doing. Poor man. He looks like a bandicoot on a burnt ridge. Is she doing the right thing? You don't want to peer or cause pain. It's just ... well ... it's just that there is also nothing worse than ignoring something as if it doesn't exist. On the other hand, a social outing is a way to get away from it all. *Get away from it all.* Huh, *that isn't* happening. The poor guy has to sit out and watch his partner dance with someone else. Humour? No, Rach! Don't be an idiot. You're not even sit-down comedian material. That could go very badly! When she asks Marianne, as you do when you care, all she says is, "It's hard and full-on, but we're both working through it."

Marianne and Kieran stay overnight at the caravan park in a cabin. She sees how breath weary he is. Why, oh why, does he choose to keep on working? Can he not see the importance of quality time together, the importance of touch? He's told her he spends periods of his day napping. It's not the pay. He's only paid for what he completes.

In the morning, Kieran takes the kayak for a paddle. It's a token gesture. He's not in much pain, but he's fatigued from the night before.

They have a trip planned for four days in March to Yangalooma Beach Resort on Finnegan's Island, a seventy-five-minute catamaran cruise from Brisbane – a gift from Kieran's boss.

As well as a check-up appointment with the stoma nurse before they leave for Brisbane, Kieran has a catch-up cuppa with three mates from soccer.

When Kieran and Marianne wake the morning after arriving at the resort, the warmth of the morning's light and the *huoh-huoh-huoh* of the seagulls infuse their beachfront room. The air smells of salt and sunlight through the open windows, and the ocean is clear blue and diamond-studded by the sun, the tide a mellow, soothing breath in ... and ... out.

There are numerous advertised extras: ATV Quad Bike Tour, Marine Discovery Cruise, Desert Safari Tour with sand tobogganing, and Snorkel the Yangalooma Wrecks. Kieran can do none of them, even though he manages to keep up with his paddling at home and the after-work beach walks with Marianne.

The mention of turtles, wobbegongs and rays puts Marianne off the snorkelling. Wobbegongs. She has no issue with carpets, but carpet sharks look disgustingly scary. She has no intention of encountering anything that can reach a length of three metres and weigh seventy kilos, thank you very much. Wikipedia is not reassuring either: '*generally* not considered dangerous to humans.' Strewth! Are they going to take a bite out of her, or not? Those ugly bearded bottom dwellers certainly have the mouth and sharp teeth to amputate a foot. She's fond of her feet – petite and perfectly lacquered.

The star attraction at the resort is the unique guest activity of hand feeding a pod of wild bottlenose dolphins who arrive at sunset of their own accord. Now, she *is* willing to have a go at that.

Kieran has such fun watching Marianne feed them. He hasn't smiled so much in a while. She looks such a sight in the waders holding a herring in her hand. The waders extend from her feet to her chest. She looks like a little kid. As she must wade at least knee-deep, she may well need to be rescued by the very same mouth she has just fed! The instructions from the staff are '*do not* touch the dolphins' and to 'hold the fish as you would an ice cream, head poking towards the sky.' That's a hoot. He can't even persuade Marianne to pick up a sardine with her fingers from a John West can, never mind suggesting which way its head should be pointing. In these fleeting moments, as he watches her, life is user-friendly. Only a slight soreness niggles at his ribs, enough to ignore.

Marianne posts a sunset photo of them on Facebook. They both look sun-and-salt-water-relaxed. Kieran is in denim shorts and a chequered shirt, and Marianne is in a denim skirt paired with a small-print floral blouse. Their poses are identical: legs crossed in front and a beer in their right hand.

On the Monday after their return, Marianne has a bad start to her working day. As it's the thirteenth of the month, she thinks perhaps it should be a Friday. When she parks in the 'reserved for staff' parking spot, she sees the resident bunny lying motionless on the concrete. She can't see any damage on the outside. She has no idea what has killed it. She triple-bags it so as not to stink out the industrial waste bin. The incident unsettles her for the rest of the day. It's a story she won't share with Kieran when she's home.

In May, Claire and Morris visit. Kieran always calls his brother-in-law Moe because of his moustache. If Moe gets caught up on his tablet with Australian stock yields, he's 'Moses'. "Hey, Moses, come down from that mountain of yours. No more talk of buy, hold and sell. It's a barbie. All I want to hear is that you've got hold of a cold beer and a steak."

Kieran now has a moniker for himself because of all the treatment he's receiving – 'The Six Million Dollar Man'. It's the title of an American sci-fi series from the seventies about an astronaut, Steve Martin, who is seriously injured when his spaceship crashes. Of course, he's handsome and athletic. Barely alive, he undergoes government-sanctioned surgery to rebuild several of his body parts with machine parts. Stoma pouches don't get a mention. Due to these implants, Steve becomes a bionic man with superhuman strength and powers. Kieran doesn't want to be stronger or faster; he wants to be *better* and not bored out of his mind most of the time. That's it. Full stop!

June is a turning point.

During a three forty-five appointment with Doctor Brysk at the oncology unit at the hospital, Kieran discovers he's dancing with demons – more tumours in the lungs.

The gunslinger has come.

Three gunshots – sudden impact, no sensation.

Stage Four. *Terminal*. Get your affairs in order.

He can taste the words, metallic, as they tingle on his lips. It's the taste of fear. Then comes the intense burn as the shrapnel from them shatters hope like a glass goblet. He takes a deep breath and digs his nails into the palms of his hands. Other than that, he remains as self-contained and silent as a coffin. He was never going to die from this. He was going to beat it. The past eighteen months of desperate hope and denial? Worthless lies.

There is no cure.

He has six to eight months to live.

For now, he will tell no one. He doesn't want to be reminded he's a dead man walking, doesn't want to see it in people's widening eyes, doesn't want to hear it in their awkward, "I am so sorry."

All Marianne can do is press her fingers into the skin of her cheeks and skid them to the groove between her lower lip and chin. She closes her eyes to the dull drumbeat of heartache. She begins to grieve. It was *never* meant to be. She knows that by mid-month there will be appointments with palliative care. She's already made an appointment with

Dave Crenell, the palliative care specialist at Clement Valley District Hospital. The Funeral Director, too. Marianne, already existing on coffee, wine, snatched sleep and a psychiatrist, is so stressed that sometimes she can't remember driving to work and back. Sometimes she loses words mid-sentence. At other times, there are heart palpitations, flutterings, dizziness. How can impending loss feel so close to falling in love? While Kieran sleeps at home, Marianne drags herself through the basic household chores.

Never one to ask questions, Kieran now asks, "How is this going to go?" The words come out with a constricted breath as if someone is kneeling on his upper chest.

Marianne tells him that his fatigue will deepen, and he will sleep a lot. She reassures him with, "I've got you. I've got us. You know that."

That night asleep, Kieran's mind lays bare what his waking mind has smothered. He dreams. At two in the morning, his breathing becomes fast and erratic with fifteen minutes of deep, fearful moaning. In the dream he's unable to cry out or scream. Burning up and shivering with fear, he wakes to feel Marianne's hand gently stroking his shoulder in a tender rhythm. She whispers in the ink-black silence, "I am here. Sleep, my darlin' man." She cradles his head between her breasts as a mother would a frightened child. He can feel the rise and fall of her chest and the warmth of her. He matches the rhythm as best he can and then, within minutes, relaxes and sleeps. To breathe together, to feel the naked freedom and intimacy of his bare flesh against hers is not to feel alone with an interior chill of otherness.

As the Saturday sun signals that it is past eight, Marianne brings him a cuppa in bed. Beneath her smile, he catches the weariness in her eyes. He does not want to leave this world, this woman. The grief of it all turns his insides to liquid, and a dribble of tears slip down his cheeks. She holds him. They cry together.

Increasingly weak, Kieran's periods of sleep are all over the place. Sometimes, midday or late afternoon, unpredictable fatigue stalls him, and he succumbs to naps that last for hours. Slumbers deep enough to dream.

Today's afternoon dream fills Kieran with a love that makes him tipsy. He and Marianne are in an empty room with a timber floor. She draws a black curtain across the back wall before they dance a duet to an audience of one, someone intent and silent. Is this an audition?

Barefooted, they dance with sensual grace and freedom. Two bodies moving through space, displacing the very air itself. Their bodies brush, intertwine, fall, rise and roll. Then, up close, close enough to kiss. Gently, he extends his arm to push her away, and as she crouches down on one knee, he pulls himself along the ground back to her, plank-like, with striding arms and legs. Still kneeling, she caresses his head and, at that moment, with no degree of separation, they meld – a living statue.

A featherlight layer of snow covers the floor. Six birch trees, bare of their leaves, cluster to the right. Kieran is bare-chested, chiselled and lean. His pre-cancerous body. Marianne is bare-legged. He lifts her, and as she glides to the ground, her feet brush snow into the air. It rises like confetti, like ashes. A kiss on the lips is held between them as their bodies pivot around each other. A caress. Then Marianne, her eyes locked on his, walks away backwards towards the birch trees. He watches, motionless. As Marianne closes her eyes, the black curtain becomes a background of bare birches where a lone bull elk stands.

The dream is familiar to him.

It is the final sensual dance scene from the movie *Pollina*.

'Why do you want to dance? Why do you want to live?'

On the first Tuesday in July, more rounds of radiate to eradicate begin: four days of radiation on his lungs. He signs his texts to Marianne, 'The Hulk'. Marianne suggests that he change the third letter to an 'n' because that is what he is to her. The Hulk, a Marvel Comics character who transforms into an enormous green humanoid monster with great strength, speed and agility due to exposure to gamma radiation. Kieran wishes! All he has to smash the bad guys is radiation's burn, fatigue, repeat.

In-between radiation appointments Kieran flies to Melbourne to see his sister, while Marianne drives north for her granddaughter's birthday.

When Kieran and Marianne return, Max flies in for a five-night visit and stays at his mother's. These are not good days. Kieran is vomiting, and his bowels are loose. He is no longer the man he was; he's a stranger to himself. The previous life he prided himself on – the early riser, the fitness freak – gone. Now, all his days and nights, a man gets up. Shits. A stoma pouch is emptied and cleaned. The man eats, showers, brushes his teeth, leaves the villa, comes back, sleeps. These are the good times before December days turn him into a lobster thrown into a pot of boiling water.

August is beach getaways up north and down south; nothing more than a two-hour drive or an hour flight.

Spring arrives with no empathy. The garden is awash with colour, sound, fragrance, movement. The yellow ball flowers of the golden wattle and the showy dazzle of the daisy blooms of the asters are a vibrant rainbow. The Crimson Rosellas are like noisy school children at recess – *cussik-cussik* – as they jostle for nectar in the 'Orange Marmalade' grevillea. The vigorous abundance of star-jasmine and milkweed perfume the breeze, and the air is aflutter with butterflies: cabbage whites, monarchs, painted ladies.

Kieran looks out at the garden with delight and despair. It blooms, buzzes, jostles, nibbles and perches, while he withers.

Max flies down at the end of August to sort out Kieran's storage shed: what needs chucking and what Max chooses to keep.

"Whatever happened to your collection of First World War gold sovereigns, Dad?"

"Your mum kept them for you." It is no matter now that with a *'You can go to hell!'* she refused to let him take them.

Mid-September and mid-October are transfers, misses, rounds of radiation, and family visits. Kieran's sixty-eighth birthday is in the mix. He celebrates with a bone scan and a barbeque with his family on the deck of Marianne's villa. Marianne convinces him to tell them his diagnosis.

"Now is the time, hun. They deserve to know, and the timing's right. We're all here, no interruptions. Is there anyone else you'd–?"

"No. No one else. Please, Marianne."

"Okay, hun. I understand."

Marianne is sure it won't be unexpected news. Poor bugger, he doesn't deserve this after all those years of managing Renata; the equivalent of driving a car with an extra-hot coffee on the dashboard and the fallout of trying not to spill a drop.

Kieran and Marianne celebrate their birthdays in the honeymoon suite at Sea Pearl Resort, a ten-minute drive from the villa on the ocean side of the highway.

Between radiation appointments, Kieran flies to Melbourne again to see his family. It allows Marianne to visit her daughter and grandkids.

Kieran continues to work – minor pain in the butt jobs – but falls asleep at his desk. He *transfers* his car (the one he bought in March last year) into Marianne's name; hers is almost twelve years old. The second week in September because of the first of six radiation treatments on his shoulder, he misses the first local dragon boat regatta since he began as sweep

Already on Endone, an immediate-release opioid, Kieran is now on Dexamethasone (a potent anti-inflammatory) to deal with the nerve pain in his shoulder. As a corticosteroid steroid, it puts some weight on him; only for him to counteract that with nausea and vomiting. He's also on Xarelto to prevent blood clots. He refers to his medications as his 'lolly bag' and Doctor David Crenell as 'Sugar Man'. And to his face, at that. They both have a laugh, as Rodriguez is a favourite of

Crenell's even though it's music from the late seventies, and he's all of thirty-four. Kieran does have a slight sweet tooth, but he has never been a pill-popper.

The palm of Kieran's right hand betrays him daily. Its hollow cups the pills he has to take, and all he can do is swallow the man he was. At least the medications are magic ships that carry him away, and add colour to days that would otherwise be dead black with pain. The only thing they don't do is take away his increasing weariness.

When Marianne's at work, her rounds of check ins by text continue.

Hi, hun. How is your day going? Did you take your 10 a.m. and 11 a.m. tablets? Do you need me to pick up any more of the anti-nausea wafers? Your daily friendly reminder service. xxx

I've been a good boy. Yes, I did, darling. No, don't need more communion wafers. A good day. I'm about to have a catch-up with six of the boys from soccer. xxoo

A good day means sweet relief from his chronic severe pain. The Endone slows down the pain signals from his central nervous system. When he develops opioid-induced constipation, Targin replaces the Endone. The paracetamol and codeine in the Panadeine Forte stop the pain messages to his brain. Together, the immediate and the long-acting opioids allow him to dance through pernicious days.

At the Aroma Mocha Cafe, Kieran and the other six only talk about hope, courage and positivity, his journey hidden behind the silence of *his* unsaid and *their* unasked. The banter is comfortable, familiar – normal.

"Running a drug cartel, are you now, Kieran? Better watch him, boys. Those flights to Melbourne, the resort holidays and the beach getaways are all a front. If any one of you tell him you've planned an overseas holiday, he'll be right in there asking if you'll carry a neat plastic package for him. Then he'll ask you to drop your daks, shove it where the sun don't shine and send you on your way."

Kieran doesn't miss a beat. "Look, Steve. You're quite capable of attracting a life sentence without any indecent, or indirect, help from me."

One of the others pips in, "We're here for you, mate. If you need to talk, we'll give you our wives' mobile numbers, won't we, boys?"

It is rounds of beer and laughter. It's a good day. A ripper of a day.

When Marianne gets home after work, she asks him how it went. "Did your soccer mates know you are seriously ill?"

"Yes. They heard it through the grapevine."

"Is that why they caught up with you?'

"Yes. All six of them were shocked because they know how fit I was."

The morning of November the eleventh at ten minutes after six is also a ripper of a day, but not in an Aussie slang way. There's an alert on Marianne's phone.

Emergency Warning – Alert Level.
Be ready to evacuate at a moment's notice.
Relocate to an urban area on the other side of the highway.
Roads may be closed without warning.

A hundred bushfires rage across New South Wales. A change in the wind, the difference between stay or go.

The landscape is one vast tinderbox. Several years of extreme drought have sucked the moisture from forests and farms. It is hotter than average, and searing winds fan strikes from dry lightning.

Two kilometres from the coast, several fires rage and roar Marianne's side of the highway; fires that require out-of-state water-bombing aircraft. Tarmac shimmies in the heat, and distant smoke rises as a funnel of moving mist and cloud that turns day skies to night. The ferocious tongues of fire are only a ten-minute drive from Marianne's villa. Her garden is full of grey ash and blackened leaves that confetti the air before settling. The air carries the stench of charred bush. Even on the safe side of the highway, the colours on the far horizon appear as an apocalyptic fiery hell of oranges, reds and yellows.

How can this be happening *now?* After all they've *been* through, all they *are* going through. The stress of having to second-guess what might happen, a destroyed home a possibility – it's a disaster movie. She rings a warm acquaintance who lives well away from the area of threat. Marianne is not the sort of person to ask favours, but she has no choice, as Kieran is stressed and weak. The cancer is devouring him in savage bites. It's metastasised to his right arm, hip, spine and some organs. He is a man relentlessly, ruthlessly and rapaciously being unmade from the inside.

"Yes, of course, you can both stay. Bring Lulu. The backyard is fenced and gated. Stay as long as you need."

Unexpectedly, the wind changes direction.

All that worry and dread for nothing.

Unfortunately, November remains a blackened month. Palliative care has now added OxyContin to Kieran's Dexamethasone and Panadol Rapid regime. Dave Crenell reassures them both with, "You're in good hands with us, Kieran. We are not about dying. We're about symptom management. My aim is to improve the quality of life for all my patients to enable them to live as well as possible. If you've got terrible nausea or pain, we've got it. We can fix it up pretty quick. One final thing. Now is the time to complete an 'Advanced Care Directive'. I know often, we don't want to face death head-on, but completing one earlier is less distressing compared to leaving it till the last minute when the patient may not be able to express their wishes, or their carer, too distressed to hear them."

For Kieran, the words are a damp firecracker. He bows his head, presses his thumbs to his eyes. His emotions tumble and tangle like an overloaded clothes dryer – betrayal, fear, agony, loss, surrender … love.

Marianne is on to the ACD the next day. She drops a copy to Kieran's doctor, the hospital and palliative care. She ensures it is on the health department's 'My Health Record' so the hospital, emergency department and ward staff have quick access. She keeps a copy at home with Kieran's other papers.

"I've become a lot of trouble to you, haven't I?"

Marianne smiles. "No, darlin'. You are my man, and I love you come what may. But while you are talking about trouble–"

"Not the toilet role issue again!"

"You betcha." Although she knows she was always peeing into the wind on that one.

It's a sky-blue December day. Summer. The heat and constant humidity seethe and drip beyond the air-con. Due to the drought and the beginning re-growth after the fires, the air teems at afternoon and dusk with the chronic tinnitus of green grocer cicadas. The discarded empty exoskeletons of the nymphs cling to tree trunks – ghosts-in-a-shell. Six to seven years underground as nymphs, and a mere six weeks free to fly, collect sap, and mate.

Kieran's cancer is now an Olympic Game competitor. It not only wants a gold medal for the one hundred metre relay event. It wants to beat the world record. On Christmas Eve, Doctor Brysk informs Kieran that he has metastases in his brain.

Always metastases.

Never metastasis – the singular.

He and Marianne have two nights booked in the honeymoon suite at Sea Pearl Resort. It's a gift from Meg and Chris from dancing, who know what a wonderful time they'd had there in August.

On the first day, Max and his fiancée, Anita, come over for a sumptuous Christmas lunch at the resort. Kieran is in a terrible way. Sadness is now part of his body, and he is sunken and sallow with fatigue and pain. If he stands, he loses his breath. Marianne knows she will have to write off a Christmas in Boondock with Kieran and her family.

When Max and Anita leave, Kieran falls into one of his deep periods of sleep. His life has become a winding sheet invisibly and indelibly inked RTS. Return to Sender.

Max is still unable to acknowledge all Marianne has done for his father. After sixteen months of Marianne caring for Kieran, Max's ill-ease and mistrust are still palpable by his remote politeness to her. To be fair to him, though, Kieran is responsible for not sharing their struggles with his son. Marianne understands why. Some men change, even on their death bed, but Kieran is not one of them. Marianne has read that people almost always die as they have lived.

All privacy gone, Kieran now requires twenty-four-hour care. The doses of pain medication are doubled. Marianne takes indeterminate leave without pay. The one thing this devouring evil has not stripped Kieran of is Marianne's love and constancy. He does not want to die forgetful; it may leave him nothing to say goodbye to.

Still, there is not a 'that's enough – *no more*' from Kieran, but there has been a shift. Now his choices are not about avoiding death. They are about gaining time.

Doctor Brysk suggests radiation of the brain.

Dave Crenell advises against radiation. There comes a time when it is wise to let go. "In the short term, the side effects include fatigue and nausea. But longer-term, the main concern is the cognitive side effects such as hearing loss, headaches, memory problems and mood swings." Before the words 'seizures' and 'paralysis' reach Dave Crenell's lips, he chokes them down.

Marianne, out of earshot of Kieran, asks Doctor Crenell a question. "What do I do if he dies at home?"

"Don't call an ambulance. If you do, the police will have to come. If it happens during the night, wait till morning, and ask Kieran's doctor to come to issue a death certificate. Then, call the undertaker."

Kieran and Marianne are at odds. He wants to go with Doctor Brysk's suggestion, Marianne with Doctor Crenell's.

A little *more* time.

More time to suffer.

Less is *more*.

Marianne tries to get Kieran to change his mind, but he is not for the turning.

The first of his three treatments is scheduled for the Wednesday before December collapses into January. On Tuesday, Claire and Morris look after Kieran in the villa while Marianne makes a hi-and-goodbye trip to drop off the Christmas presents to her grandkids. Before she leaves, Kieran asks Morris for help. "I'd really appreciate you helping Max see to my tax return and pay any overdue accounts. He's at sea with it all, Moe – bamboozled."

"Sure thing, Kieran. I'll take care of it."

Marianne returns home on Thursday afternoon. When she sees Kieran, it is she who says, "That's enough, *No More!* I don't want you to die, but I don't want this."

Kieran is a zombie. Brain fried, he stares blankly into space. He's unable to keep up with a conversation. Unable to put three words together. Unable to speak without slurring.

Marianne cancels the remaining two sessions of radiation.

Kieran's intensive treatment over sixteen months has been inefficient and cruel. His remaining eight months will be made up of six million breaths. Breaths that will become shallow and irregular with long pauses of seconds or a minute.

He's now in a large hospital bed with a manoeuvrable configuration.

The living room has become a hospital ward.

Money, That's What I Want

"Geez, Morris, is that how much my father has in his Super?"

"Yes, Max. Happy New Year! It shows the power of saving from young, patience and being on the frugal side. If I organise a 'Binding Death Benefit Nomination' form and a new 'Power of Attorney' naming you, all that is in Kieran's estate will be left to you. That way, money can be drawn-down before probate. As there is little money other than in his Self-Managed Super Fund, it will make your dad's Will null and void. It'll also save about thirteen thousand dollars in tax once the estate settles."

"But he's so zonked out on morphine; can we do this without his consent? The 'before probate', I mean?"

"Sure. Your dad's not one to sniff at such a significant saving, even if it's of no direct benefit to him. Also, it allows you to decide if you think someone he's been with such a short time deserves the generous one hundred thousand dollars he's promised her in his Will."

Max says nothing. Morris has a point.

Morris has a few too many wines over a home-cooked meal by Marianne that Friday night. As the saying goes, if you want to find out something that someone else would rather you didn't, 'a drunk man's words are a sober man's thoughts'.

It comes out what Morris plans to do.

"Morris, without Kieran's knowledge, that's *so* wrong. All he asked you to do was help Max to pay some accounts and lodge his tax return. What about the money Kieran wants me to have? You know I've used up all my leave – sick, holiday, long service – to look after Kieran, and I've also stopped work to care for him. He doesn't want me to be in a precarious position after he dies, as he knows I won't stay in this villa after he's gone, and I'll have the cost of selling and rebuying."

Neither Claire, Morris nor Max has asked how she's coping. For weeks she's been accidentally breaking things. Her fingers touch objects but are unable to holdfast. The first was a cheap polka dot cereal bowl from K-Mart her grandkids gave her one birthday. Then there was the crystal wine glass. Glass shards scattered in places in the kitchen you'd think they would never reach.

"You'll have to sort that out with Max now. We're Kieran's family. It's decided."

Does Morris seriously think she doesn't know what the two of them are up to?

Indifferently polite to her face and then stabbing her in the back and betraying Kieran's wishes.

"Marianne, I'm taking over my father's financial affairs from now on. Please do not use his bank account or cards to pay for anything. Also, if you use your money to buy anything for him without running it by me first, I won't reimburse you."

"For god's sake, Max, do you know what you're asking? I have enough stress at the moment without sweating the small stuff. I've put my well-being on the line to do the very best for your dad. Do you know what my psychiatrist said when Kieran was diagnosed three months after we'd been living together? 'You do have the choice to end this relationship.' I didn't because I love your dad, and I'm as loyal as they come. Sadly, you can't see that. To be treated as if I'm not to be trusted is incredibly hurtful."

Max says nothing beyond, "Where is Kieran's wallet?"

Fool that she is, she meekly retrieves it from Kieran's bedside drawer and hands it to Max.

Max flips it open. It has three fifties, a couple of twenties and a ten, and receipts for purchases Marianne has made on Kieran's behalf. He empties it and gives the wallet back to her.

The assault doesn't stop there.

"Morris and Claire also think I should hold 'Power of Attorney' instead of you."

Marianne is so full of anger; it is all that stops her from bursting into tears. They so don't trust her. They stay at her place, smile, eat her meals and then, do this. Worse is that they are doing it to a dying man who should not be worried by such things.

When Kieran has a better day, she tells him what has happened. That Morris and Max intend to alter the 'Power of Attorney' and secure a 'Binding Beneficiary Nomination' so as to allow Max to withdraw all the money before his dad is dead and buried and to cut Marianne out as a beneficiary. There is only one word for what they plan to do – heartless.

"They would never do that, Marianne. You must have misunderstood."

"Hun, I did not misunderstand. There is only one way to sort it out. We need to speak with your solicitor, Lee. If you're okay with that, I can arrange a three-way phone conference."

Lee cancels a meeting to speak to them straight away.

Lee advises that if Kieran wants to protect Marianne and his financial wishes, he must withdraw the money immediately as a lump sum. "If you do that, I can draw up a new Will with Marianne off it. Also, Kieran, *do not* sign anything Max or Morris give you without consulting with me first."

That afternoon Max is back in town.

"Dad, I have the 'Binding Beneficiary Nomination' form from your accountant, so there's no need for you to go to the meeting on Tuesday the fourteenth. You just need to sign it, and I'll take it back to him. He's also advised me to transfer the estate from your name to mine."

Marianne speaks up. "Max, that's not so. This form is the one Morris organised with you last time you were here."

Kieran shoots a look at Max. "Is that so, Max?"

"No, Dad." A stainless-steel look ricochets in Marianne's direction. "*It's not.*"

He's a little too adamant, so Kieran asks, "You're my son, Max. I hope I can trust you."

Max looks him straight in the eye, "Yes, you can."

"Okay. Gentleman to gentleman, let's shake on it."

They shake.

When Max leaves, Marianne can barely contain her fury. Max has made her look a fool and a liar.

She rings Kieran's accountant, Bruce, on speaker-phone so that Kieran can hear. "Is that what happened, Bruce? Is that exactly how it went down?"

"No, it's not. Max brought a copy of what he wanted and asked me to type it up on my letterhead. Said he'd get his father to sign it and bring it back. From an accountancy point of view, the request was above board."

"Thanks for clarifying things, Bruce. Goodbye."

"Happy to help. Bye."

Marianne wishes she could spare Kieran all of this, but she cannot allow Max to make a liar of her in front of the man who loves her. "You do understand that Max as your Legal Personal Representative plans to cut me out as a beneficiary?"

"Max would never do that."

Marianne doesn't argue. "It's lovely that you feel that way about Max."

To appease Marianne, Kieran does as Lee advised.

After the call, Marianne rings Max to ensure he has no excuse to accuse her of playing his game.

"Hi, Max. Just letting you know that your dad has spoken to his accountant and solicitor. On their advice, and in line with his wishes, he's withdrawn the money he wants me to have and has given it to me. It simplifies things for everyone concerned so we all know where we stand." Sure does, you conniving little shit. "I'll email you a copy of the new Will and the 'Power of Attorney' in your name."

There's silence at the end of the line. Max knows he's been outmanoeuvred. "Okay. Got it. Thanks." He puts the phone down.

Money and Wills.

They bring out the worst in some people.

Blacker than Black

It's the thirteenth of January. It doesn't involve a Friday or a dead rabbit, but it does involve two double-dealers in the dining room. It's a Monday at eleven in the morning, and Kieran is in a deep sleep.

"If you don't work, Marianne, you can't support yourself. Morris and I have decided to look after Kieran. Take him to Melbourne."

As they are both retired, Marianne assumes they will care for Kieran in their own home.

"Oh, no. We couldn't cope. We'd need to put Kieran in the palliative care section of the hospital."

"I'm sorry, Claire, that's not happening. Kieran and I want to be together with the little time we have left. Don't you get it? Look at Kieran. Your brother has weeks to live. You'd do that to him? Uproot him from all he knows – me, his friends, the Silver Chain nurses who look after him with gentle humour and care. I'm not going to allow you to do that to him just to make the point that you consider me an outsider and not Kieran's new partner."

The shock, the fury, further mobilise her tongue. "You two are a piece of work. You should be ashamed of yourselves. Time for you to leave – *now*."

She wants nothing to do with them.

They fly out the following day.

Three days later, Kieran is in hospital. Stressed, he has a high temperature and an infection. The hospital transfers him to palliative care.

Renata visits Kieran on the second day. For herself, and Max's sake, she's come to make peace with a dying man.

"In the early days, we made a brilliant goal-oriented team: you careful and systematic, me instinctive and impulsive. I regret that, overtime, we did not lead each other into being the best each of us could be. I'm deeply sorry that by becoming so unloving, I robbed you of your ease and playfulness, even perhaps contributed to your illness. I am deeply ashamed of that, Kieran. Please forgive me."

"I forgive you. It means a lot you came. Let's let bygones be bygones." It is all he has the energy to say.

Back home after four days, he's dropped another level – bed *after* breakfast, hours of sleep. He continues to do what he has done for months, cough and spit up blood – lumps of it.

"Don't let me sleep more than an hour or two."

Marianne nods, but they both know he'll be in a unawakenable sleep. If only this were a fairy tale. She'd wake him with a kiss, and they'd live happily ever after. In hindsight, it was never going to be that way – red flags are always green when you're in love.

By late January, Kieran knows it's the start of the end, daylight sleeps of five to six hours. It's a massive effort for him to speak, not just because of the breathing, but because up until this moment, he has used all his energy to suppress the one thought that has plagued his mind for eighteen months. He's afraid his voice will fail him. "I'm dying, aren't I?"

The words are pineapple rind in his mouth.

"Yes, my darlin' man. You are. Anything you need to let me know now before that time comes?"

"I don't want to die alone and in silence. I want to listen to the four of you talking to me. Snuggle next to me and hold my hand. I want the feeling I had as a kid when the dentist gave me happy gas for an extraction: the warm fade of going under as the voices of the dentist and the dental assistant dissolved."

She hugs him. For a petite woman, she gives the best hugs. Hugs that make everything alright.

"I'll make us a cuppa, hun."

"A couple of digestives with that?" He smiles. Digestive biscuits and a hot cuppa. As good as a hug when things are difficult.

As she waits for the kettle to boil, her gaze fixes on Kieran's walking stick propped in the corner by the front door. For the past weeks, he's joked about how he might need it. The truth is that there is no door he can walk through now. When he moves around the house, he dawdles, bent at the knees – once up, do not stop. His breath is erratic and brings severe pain. For Marianne, it is déjà vu of her dad's final days.

She rings Max and Claire. "I think you'd better come. I don't think Kieran will last much longer. He's drowsy and weak. No energy."

With Marianne driving, she and Kieran pick Max up from the airport. A ten-thirty arrival. Saturday, February the fifteenth. Max chats about where he and his dad can go for coffee and breakfast tomorrow and what they'll do after. At thirty-three, this man-boy has no idea.

When they disembark at home, Max notices how his father struggles to walk from the car to the front door. The shrivel and fade a cruel magic trick.

Once inside, Kieran struggles to stay awake.

Today is the last day food will pass his lips. Two of his favourites. A pork roast dinner and apple crumble.

By Monday he is sleeping so much, both day and night, that Marianne has to empty his stoma pouch while he sleeps – the urine is minimal.

His body is shutting down.

A day later, he doesn't want his morning tablets. He's incapable of swallowing them.

"Max, could you try to persuade your dad." She knows it won't work, but she wants Max to feel included.

"Dad, you need to take these. They'll take the pain away from your shoulder and hip."

The man in the bed shakes his head, a man who no longer looks like Max's father. Max takes a deep breath, turns, and charges for the bathroom. All Marianne can hear from in there is the vanity taps on full bore.

Marianne rings Vicky the palliative care nurse who comes twice a week.

"Hi, Vicky. I know you're due today, but we need you now. Kieran's unable to take his medication. He's highly distressed, as he's soiled himself and won't let me, or his son, change him."

"Don't you worry, my lovely. Dave and I will be there faster than a speeding ambulance."

God, what would Marianne do without Vicky's cheery matter-of-factness and compassion? Marianne can't allow herself to weep, to scream. She looks upwards so the liquid that rims her lower eyelids doesn't overspill.

When Vicky and Dave Crenell arrive, Max excuses himself. "I need some air. I'll be back in fifteen."

He walks over to the nearby reserve. If he were back in Melbourne, he'd put heavy metal music all the way up and howl – fuck the neighbours. There's no dignity in a death like this. Is that what death is? A sadist's taunt that you've reached the end of your shelf-life, your 'best before' date, your 'use by date' – damaged, deteriorated, perished. Max's sadness rages. His head throbs, and a current of pins and needles prick his body. *Fuck it!* He lets out a guttural scream. The large dogs in the neighbourhood howl. He doesn't care who's heard him, who's looking. He bends down and splashes his face with creek water. Okay, Max. Get yourself together. He lies down on the grass, takes deep breaths – five in, hold for ten, out for twenty.

Calm and in control, he heads back to the villa.

Back inside, his father has pepped up. Saline drip. Blood pressure and pulse monitor. Morphine. He's clean and looking comfortable.

Dave Crenell and Vicky remain in the villa all morning.

Vicky turns to Max. "Of all my patients, your dad never complains. And believe you me, my days are full of the whingers, the bellyachers, the cry-babies, the moaners, the grumblers, the snivellers and the squawkers, and that's just my six kids and my husband." Vicky turns to Marianne. "Remember, love. You've done a fantastic job through all this. He's approaching the end now – a day or two. I think he should be in the hospice. Let them do the looking after, and you do the loving."

'Fantastic job.' No. Marianne feels *so* powerless. *So* heartbroken she's unable to make this go away, make him better again. "I can't, Vicky. It's not what he wants. A heartfelt thank you as always. You're a treasure."

When Marianne closes the door, she turns and sees Max looking at her. It's a look she hasn't seen before.

Max is in pause, re-think, re-record. What were Claire and Morris thinking of, removing his father from this loving care? And, when he came back from the bathroom a while back, he heard Vicky call Marianne 'my lovely' on the phone. At last, the chink of light is now a spotlight on the untruths his mother has spun about Marianne, and that Claire and Moe have buzzed into head-on. They've got it all wrong.

That night Marianne sleeps on the lounge. Kieran makes noises on and off the entire night. Max comes out from the spare room a few times to check on his father.

Kieran is semi-comatose.

On the morning of Wednesday the nineteenth, the doorbell rings. It's Claire and Morris. Marianne is in the kitchen making snacks. Max, red-eyed but in control, opens the door. Marianne has arranged chairs around the bed. Kieran is in a deep coma but still breathing.

After saying a hello, Claire's next words are, "I hoped I'd be able to speak to him."

She's upset, so Marianne tries to soothe her. "Claire, they say hearing is the last to go. We can talk to him as much as we want; include him in the conversation. I'm sure he'll hear you." It's the first time Marianne has seen a flicker of gratitude in Kieran's sister's eyes. "Feel free to say whatever comes into your mind, Claire."

At that moment, the four of them are united. It's all about Kieran now.

They sit, wine and beer in hand. Marianne, Claire, Morris and Max. Lulu is lying on the bed next to Kieran's feet. Marianne orders a home delivery Indian meal. The spices warm the room. A partial antidote to the sadness in, and around, all five of them.

Marianne starts the conversation. "You know, he never complained. Never asked the question, why me."

Claire turns to her husband. "He always took things on the chin, didn't he, Morris?"

"Yes. I think we'd all agree on that."

Claire continues. "Kieran, do you remember when we were kids – always fighting? You know, the usual stuff between siblings two years apart. Anyway, our parents always tried to broker the peace. Mother was more patient than Father. She would beg and plead for us to get on. Father was a man of action, few words. Remember, Kieran, that day when we were arguing on a long car trip to the beach and Mother was driving? Father, as a last resort, reached round and swatted us on the knees with a rolled-up newspaper. We continued fighting as savagely as only kids could.

'*Gimmie it!*'

'*No*, it's *mine!*'

He leant right over, ripped the toy out of our haggling clutches, and tossed it through his open window. We never did fight after that."

They all add a story of their own. But in the still silences between, Kieran's inert body is the oppressive form that stings like an open wound doused with iodine. The laboured rasping in and out. By one-thirty in the afternoon, he has slipped further. Ragged breaths. Stops and starts.

The meal finished, Max opens a bottle of port that his father has kept for a gulp past fifteen years – a Taylor's Quinto de Terra Feita Vintage Port 2005. The label is flawless. His dad, a man of supreme patience, would only have opened this port as close to the 'drink to' date as possible.

Max hopes the cork won't fall apart at the sight of the corkscrew.

The four of them toast Kieran and share what they love about him the most.

At five-past-two in the afternoon, Kieran's eyebrows slacken, his eyelids flutter, and he drifts away on morphine with Marianne snuggled next to him holding his hand. Then comes the moment when his chest fails to rise and fall. It is a dagger that plunges into the skin of the afternoon. Death has taken a man, a partner, a father, a brother, a brother-in-law, a dog's best friend.

Kieran looks as if he's dozing – pristine and peaceful. It is a quiet end. He floats on a calm ocean as warm as sunlight. No more fear. No more pain.

Marianne kisses him on the forehead, her lips a salty, "I will *always* love you". Love smells of sweetness and stench. It would have been their third anniversary five days later – leather. A tactile symbol of the durable, the secure. Tributaries of tears bathe her and Kieran's clasped hands. Claire takes her brother's other hand and kisses it; a single tear rolls onto the middle knuckle of her right hand.

Lulu jumps off the bed, her head down. She avoids the lounge she used to sit on next to Kieran. She will evade it for three months.

No one speaks.

The sound of grief has no words.

Max takes control and rings the doctor and the funeral parlour. Only after that do any of them pay heed to the day outside, and the slick hum of cars on the rain-wet tarmac. As the rain clears, the late afternoon sunshine glints through the gaps between the slats of the vertical blinds revealing dancing dust motes.

PART FOUR

With and Without You

Marianne is grateful she can give Kieran a proper funeral. A Celebration of Life. The arrangements anaesthetise her from the tsunami of grief that threatens to incapacitate her.

If the funeral had been five weeks later amid a Public Health Emergency, it would have been limited to ten people, including the funeral director and his staff, with a four-metre square social distancing during the service. No additional people outside. Polite reminders, 'Sir, you're getting too close ... please stand at least an arm's distance away.' Ah! Social distancing. Had Kieran been in care, he would have died with not a single loved one close by in his last moments.

Marianne is also grateful that the torrential rain that has continued for days, and is predicted to continue on the funeral day, ceases. The grass is a saturated sponge, but the sun is out.

Liam, Molly, and Ana are there as support for Marianne. The room is brimming with people: Max and Anita; Claire and Morris; Pete; Col; Kieran's sporting friends; dancing buddies; Kieran's boss.

Invited, Renata is missing.

Rachel is aware of the uselessness of words. The well-meaning platitudes that, when said, sound inane. *I'm so sorry for your loss.* She notices some say nothing at all. Understandable, that. There are no perfect words when someone's life has been torn asunder by loss. You only hope they see in your eyes that you acknowledge and understand. She says the six words anyway.

Marianne delivers her eulogy, her daughter by her side if she can't continue.

"Thank you, Kieran, for showing me what true love *really* is. May the angels hold you safely, my darlin' man, until we can be together once more and dance eternally ever after.

I loved Kieran, and he loved me. Not a day went by without him telling me that he loved me. He was a very affectionate man, and trust and loyalty meant a lot to him.

I wish with all my heart that I could close my eyes, open them, and see him here beside me. That I could reach out and touch him, hear his laugh. See him smile. It's all the more challenging because my dad, who Kieran reminded me of in many ways, died at almost the same age.

Anyway, now both have vanished from my life but not my heart. My world is empty without Kieran, my sweet, sweet man who was always so willing to please. I miss so many things about him not being here.

I miss ...
coming home to his long cuddles and kisses.
I miss ...
my head resting in the crook of his neck.
I miss...
the eye contact that we always had.

I miss...

his smile and cheeky humour.

I miss...

sitting together on the couch, chatting, watching TV or listening to music.

I miss ...

how he always turned on the bedside lamps at night before we went to bed.

I miss ...

hearing him singing in the shower.

I love you, Kieran. *You* will be part of *me*, forever."

There is a slide show to the song 'Dancing in the Sky' by Dani and Lizzy. There are no slides of Max, Renata and Kieran together.

Once the day is over, Marianne is like someone on a treadmill on the top setting brought to a forcible stop by the press of a button. She feels incredibly lost. Alone.

That night, as the light from the bedside lamp falls as a soft haze of warm white around her, she drifts into sleep. Her dad visits her. She feels the depression in the mattress on Kieran's side as her dad sits on the edge of the bed. He watches her. He says nothing. In the morning, longing fills her, a nostalgia for the comfort of a dimple in the mattress.

Unlike Kieran, work is not the best distraction for her. Patients complain about minor aches and pains. The unempathetic lurches up in her. She wants to say, "Be grateful you're alive. I just lost the man I love." She can't even make it through till morning tea. She's an automaton.

Ashes

One cry-baby-cry afternoon a month after the funeral, Marianne begins to sort out Kieran's belongings. Inside the urn, all that was Kieran is in a twist-tied clear plastic bag. All seventy-five kilos of him melted away in a flash fire; the tumours – blackened coral – the last to burn as a gold glow amongst the ashes. No genie in a bottle. No three wishes. No fairy-tale ending.

The bag is tagged with a stainless-steel disc inscribed with a six-digit number. The contents are not what Marianne expects. Not black or brown. The beige-coloured contents are identical to beach sand with large white flecks of seashell.

Hollow beyond tears, Marianne aches with emptiness. Sometimes she escapes the crushing grief, but *always* it waits for her. It's a predator in tall grass that she stumbles into. She's blindsided by a bottle in the kitchen cupboard (Benadryl cough syrup), by a song by Human Nature on the radio.

Longing is the double helix of grief. Missing the scent of him, she finds an echo of it in his sports bag – a T-shirt, a bottle of body wash. She holds the armpits of the T-shirt to her nostrils and breathes deeply.

The sad do foolish things.

They hang on to ghosts.

The villa has become a grim time capsule inside which silence and sadness slink.

One unbidden morning, as Marianne looks out at the sun streaming through her open living-room window, she knows she cannot live in this villa, this town. It holds too much of their life together. She needs to sell up and move. Jump off the cliff into a new life. Move north close to her daughter and her grandchildren, close to the vibrant rock 'n' roll culture of Langaratta. It's okay for her to start a new life on her own. She'll be fine. There is no need for her to jump into someone else's canoe. There's another realization, too. She does not have the reserves to repeat this odyssey with anyone else.

Before Marianne moves, Max and Anita visit one last time to collect the ceramic cremation urn. The three of them have afternoon tea at the villa. No, Max does not want any of Kieran's belongings. But, for the first time, and with warmth, he says, "Thank you for all you did for my father." He does not want to stay in touch; he needs to tend to himself and his mother.

Also, it remains raw for Max how adrift he was at the funeral. He was an intruder among a room filled with strangers, the wooden lectern, a witness stand at a trial. He noticed the looks during his short emotional speech. He knew his words came across as cold and distant. What the hell did they expect? Some people are better at one-to-one than amongst a crowd of strangers. Besides, his one wish was that his father had left this life as 'Best friend and soulmate to Renata, father to Max'.

As the months pass, Marianne doesn't want the slippage of memory. She wants her memories resistant to the fade and fray of creeping amnesia, so she tends them, keeps all their text messages, letters, notes, photographs. She repeats to herself and others the story that was hers and Kieran's; she gift wraps it around what her heart wants to remember.

She shares, commemorates, reminisces and then, *the day*. The day when her grief is no longer a deep, gaping wound that heals slowly and bleeds at the slightest touch. It becomes a papercut. An inner voice whispers to her, *You were never meant to be together for the rest of your lives.* Life brought him to her as his last chance to reprioritise and discover he was worthy of love.

On the day Marianne leaves the villa for the last time, as she closes the sliding door to the deck, there's a butterfly with vibrant turquoise-blue, black-edged wings shaped like a kite. She's sure she's seen such butterflies over spring and summer moving from flower-to-flower feasting on nectar, seldom at rest. Even when settled, their wings, vertical, vibrating constantly.

The butterfly looks as if it's caught between the glass and the flyscreen, facing outward to a day it cannot reach. She slides open the flyscreen and then the glass door. Still, it stays. She blows a faint breeze of a breath over it. When it alights from the glass and gauze as a fast-flying blue flash, it is as if a piece of the sky has taken flight.

A life measured in weeks, not years.

Yes, life is too short *not to* be happy.

Acknowledgements

I HAVE AN ANECDOTE TO SHARE before I acknowledge the behind-the-scenes extras who have contributed to *For the Love of Kieran* at the pre-publication stage.

A female acquaintance who read my first novella, *Searching for North*, approached me and remarked, 'Hallelujah! I've found myself a female surfing partner.'

I completely understood why she thought that, but it was as far from the truth as the possibility of discovering a surfboard in the middle of the Simpson Desert. It was a writer's magic trick! How had I pulled it off? I had sought the help of a keen surfer and trawled for authentic jargon and details. Who was that person? My son. The question-and-answer session was as bonding as it was helpful.

So, here's to the 'extras' who contributed to *For the Love of Kieran*.

I thank Wendy Young who willingly checked the sections relating to dragon boat racing. Your tweaks were only minor, but they made a significant difference to the tone and authenticity of those sections.

Likewise, I thank Nick Lambert (a local teacher and passionate environmentalist) who gave me a snippet of his time to chat about butterflies and cicadas local to the area, and the antics blokes get up to on camping trips.

I thank a casual social friend – you know who you are – for wanting a fictionalised memoir of the journey she went through with the man she loved. I am grateful for the trust you placed in me, assured I would honour your story, and that you embraced my need to blur the boundaries of fact and fiction for dramatic effect. That you were thrilled with the result was praise enough.

I raise a glass of red to my two beta readers, Chris Carter and Lanae Shipply, for your time, clear thinking, and contribution to the 'at a distance space' that, together with resting a manuscript well, are invaluable to a writer at the final draft stage.

I so greatly value the contribution of Evan Cilento of Green Avenue Design for the cover and typesetting. Evan, you are a dream to collaborate with and forever generous with your clear thinking, creative input, and patience with a Goldilocks and her 'just right' porridge.

I am most grateful to the author Leone Sperling who cast her editing eye over my work. Your wonderfully forthright suggestions improved the strength of the narrative when sections of my writing became didactic, unconvincing, confusing, ineffective or overdone. In the main, I accepted and applied your suggestions.

I thank the diversity of the many novellas I have read and what my in-depth analysis of them has contributed to my writing. I have a deep affection for the novella as a literary form that has a long and illustrious tradition. When I speak to readers, I am dismayed that the novella – approximately fifteen to fifty thousand words – is often unheard of or underrated. Yet, today when many of us are time-poor, the novella (a one hour to three hours read at an average speed) has even more relevance than ever – it packs a punch in a small package.

I thank my parents and the generations before them; all of whom have contributed to my DNA. I am courageous, curious and always up for a creative challenge. These three traits combined led me on a journey to complete a novella almost three times the length of *Searching for North*, with the added complexities that involved.

Lastly, to readers everywhere, of whatever genre, consider yourselves heartily thanked. Without you, a book is but a one-way conversation.

Alina